10 Dates

Emily James

Emily James

Editing by: Randie Creamer

This novel is written using the author's birth tongue, U.K.
English.
If you would like to purchase the translation rights, please email
the author directly: emilyjames.author@gmail.com
ISBN-13: 978-1521308608

DEDICATION

For David—who makes me laugh every single day.

CONTENTS

Chapter 1

New Year's Eve

I'm beginning to regret coming to this awful, chintzy golf club, housing more pensioners than you can bash with a bingo board. Not that I'm ageist, or whatever the politically correct term is. It's just that I had hoped for a more intimate and romantic location for Chris, after three long years, to declare his love for me and to finally propose. After all, he promised that as soon as his dating app was up and running, I would be his number one priority. Now that it's been up and running for the last two years, tonight is my night.

"Joan, did you get a cake?" Chris hollers, an octave above the sound of George Michael crooning about last Christmas. He knows that I hate being called Joan, but he thinks it's cute to shorten my name to my grandmother's title.

"Of course, baby," I reply, not letting it spoil my mood. I plaster on a smile, while I frantically search the room.

I've been so busy mentally preparing myself for his proposal, albeit by swigging back large gulps of wine, I completely forgot all about the sodding cake.

"You did remember the cake? My baby needs cake. Please tell me you remembered." Chris dramatically palms his face as if he can't quite believe that he trusted me with this momentous task.

"Babe, I have the cake, don't worry." I wink at Chris and the creases lining his forehead relax.

"I'm sorry, it's just, you know how important tonight is." Pride gleams from his eyes and I smile. I can't believe I've been so nervous.

"I love you," I tell him.

"I'll be right back," Chris says, heading off to the bar.

I start to rummage through my bag to try to find my to-do list. I've been stressed and forgetful since Chris dropped tonight's party on me three weeks ago. I've been so busy organizing the food, the music, and the venue, I'm scared the cake slipped my mind. Normally, I would have been annoyed at being expected to organise and pay for everything but since this is our engagement party (well, it will be once he actually proposes), it only seems right I pay my fair share. Not forgetting, Chris must have had to fork out for the engagement ring, which is probably why my Christmas stocking was more like a sock.

I get excited when my hands find a crumpled piece of paper, only to find it's the receipt for the entertainment: Naughty Nineties. It was the best I could get at short notice.

I look around and check, wondering if I even did order a cake. Chris catches my eye and shakes his head, throwing me the, 'You're so crazy' eyes, and then he goes back to schmoosing with some work colleagues and investors he's invited along to the party. Never one to miss an opportunity, Chris has invited anyone and everyone in the app, entrepreneur, and marketing business. He is determined that—Sexy Talk Dating—will take over the world. Although after four years of him trying to make it a success, even I am starting to wonder if it will ever gain traction. I wash away the thought with another slug of wine.

"Melinda," I hiss to my best friend, who's finally back from her bathroom break. I still cannot believe she managed to find a babysitter for her ever-expanding brood, especially on the hottest night of the year, but then she is fully aware how important tonight is to me. "Did you get the cake?" I check, even though I know Mrs. Organised would never forget such a detail.

All my emails go through Melinda; she just signs in, and adds any of my to-do's to her to-do list. She likes to organise and I, well, tend to forget, so she just pencils me on the calendar next to Tegan's ballet and Jakey's braces, and I never forget anything anymore. Simple.

Melinda used to be a Personal Assistant before she had her four children. Now she has an advanced degree in time management and crowd control as the Sergeant Major of her family home (and my life). She can whip even the most complicated or unruly task into perfect and organised calm. It is just one of the many reasons that I love her.

Melinda points a red manicured nail that matches her tight red dress over to a big square box that's near the buffet that was demolished hours ago.

I hold my hands together and pray a thank you to her.

"As if I would forget. Joanie, you're finally going to get married. It's what you've always wanted, ever since you were a little girl. I just hope you don't look too drunk on the photos when he finally proposes. You must have sunk a bottle and a half of wine waiting for him." Melinda taps at her watch and drains the rest of her glass.

There's now four empty wine bottles on our table, which is why I'm feeling a little less nervous and more than a little inebriated. It's nearly eleven p.m. and the waiting is killing me. Chris still needs to say his speech and propose before the strike of midnight, when all our guests will want to raise a glass to toast our good news and then welcome in the New Year to the pre-recorded sound of Big Ben's chimes. It's how he always said he would do it, just as soon as the app was live, and we were in 'the right place.'

Of course, the first year the app launched it was too soon to focus on marriage, because when we did get married, Chris wanted to focus solely on our relationship. See, Chris is a forward-thinker; he wants to make sure the future is bright for us, that I'm well looked after when we get married and have a family. Just recently I have come to realise that the time is now and the proposal is well on its way. After all, he as good as said it when he moved in with me and sold his flat, 'freeing up some more cash.'

I take the last sip from my glass. "I'm going to slow down now," I tell Melinda as I top up both our glasses. "It's my nerves; they're making me thirsty."

I look at my watch, again. The faux gold is already chipping from around the face, even though I've only had it since Christmas day. It was a gift from Chris and is almost identical to the one I wanted. He calls it the 'cost effective version,' even with me having bought him the MacBook that he actually wanted.

Melinda studies me and takes a measured sip of her wine. Her hair is cut in a functional, low maintenance bob that somehow emphasises her set of enormous breasts that just won't quit being perky and bouncy despite them having fed four kids.

"It's not too late to change your mind, you know. We could leg it out of here, take that bottle of champagne over there and just go. The mother-in-dragon isn't bringing my terrorists back until tomorrow, so we could totally escape, change our identities, run away—I would help you, so long as we're back at my place by dinner time." Melinda jokes, at least I think she does.

It's fair to say that she is not Christopher Morris' biggest fan. In fact, she makes no secret of the fact that she doesn't like him, and she mocks him at every opportunity.

I think it began when Chris cheated on me with my upstairs neighbour, Barbara, back when we first got together. In Chris's defence, we had only been together two weeks and he was on a lads' night out, but still, Melinda takes no prisoners when it comes to loyalty. What Melinda doesn't see is Chris's passion and dedication. I mean, in some ways she does have a point, a lads' night out is no excuse for cheating, but he was very sorry, and he has made up for it ever since. He doesn't even make eye contact with my neighbour anymore. Melinda often jokes that Chris's app is crap but she doesn't get that it's a tough market, and Chris has invested every penny he has in it. I just hope he knows when to move on and work on something else.

"Shots o-clock!" Mikey, our rogue third-wheel sings as he places a tray with too many shots to count onto the table in front of us. Mikey climbs over and swings his hips in order to squeeze in between Melinda and me. As he attempts to part the Red Sea, a scattering of glitter rains down on us from Mikey's glitter ball white shirt.

Mikey is camp like a row of tents and, quite rightly, makes no apologies for it! Melinda and I both adore him for his fierce and fun ways. Tonight, for example, Mikey is wearing tight leather trousers and his shirt is unbuttoned just enough to provide a teaser at his rock-hard pecs underneath. He wears his highlighted hair in a soft, swept up quiff, which he calls a flat-twist Mohawk. Mikey doesn't usually do carbs, but he's making an exception tonight as he takes a swig of his wine. He's high maintenance, and not at all what you might expect for a high-ranking pilot.

Chris had waggled his brows and rolled his eyes when he saw what Mikey was wearing tonight, but I think it's because he struggles to understand him. It doesn't help that Mikey flirts outrageously with Chris, and in response Chris jerks and leaps from whichever direction Mikey attacks. He then usually sprints from the building as if it's on fire, flustered and embarrassed.

"How many shots did you fucking buy?" Melinda yells at Mikey as she gleefully rubs her hands together.

I look over at Chris, to check he didn't hear her use bad language. Chris doesn't agree with women swearing, and I know it will totally piss Melinda off if he so much as tuts in her direction. I'm safe though, he's still chatting to a local radio station host, topping up their champagne. They seem to be drinking the good stuff, unlike me, Melinda, and Mikey.

"I'm sorry, but this party blows, and not in a good way." Mikey passes me a tongue-in-cheek grin.

I nod. "I can't even defend my own engagement party." I sigh. "It's not at all what I expected."

Back when Chris emailed me to announce we were having a party, I eagerly replied with a list of everyone who needed to be here tonight. My parents retired to Spain when I went to University. Sadly, they won't be witnessing my special moment. I had planned to video call them, but it seems this place is a black hole for Internet connection. Either that or, when I decided to wear my contact lenses tonight—so I'd look better in the photos—I didn't take into account that my eyes would water like little cry babies and my thumbs would refuse to coordinate with the touch screen on my phone.

"I need to be drunk to cope with this," Mikey tells us as he pushes dark, evil looking shots towards us. "I mean, who invited these people. Suit over there looks like he just got sprung from the funeral home," Mikey points, yelling across the table.

I let out an involuntary giggle because he's not wrong. "That's just Chris's dad, and he does work at a funeral home, which, by the way," I lower my voice knowing I can get a bit rowdy after a few drinks, "is why Chris and I both have such excellent funeral plans."

This information is too much for Mikey and Melinda

and they both start to fizzle and spit with laughter. Melinda smacks her hand on the table and Mikey hugs himself. They snort loudly and it attracts a few glances.

After I stop giggling, I nudge them both. "Come on, I'm getting engaged soon. That man will be my father-in-l… oh no…"

I down my shot in one and Mikey places another straight in its place, which I suck down too.

Chris's dad is a serious drawback to our relationship. Still, I think, not everyone sees their in-laws regularly. Perhaps we could move…

Melinda and Mikey each do a shot too, and then the nineties mishmash of Christmas pop songs is replaced by static as Chris hits the microphone with his hands.

As he stands, slightly shorter than average, on the small raised platform in front of the buffet, I think back to what first attracted me to him.

It had been a rough night. Another long-term boyfriend had just dumped me. I was feeling unattractive and unappreciated. Chris had walked into the bar in his black suit, the same suit he's wearing now, his 'lucky suit,' he calls it. He'd flattered and complimented me and told me all about his app idea. He was impressed I had my own place, a plush apartment that my grandparents left me. I had a full-time job and stood on my own two feet. I might only work in accounts, but he respected my dedication to turn up on workdays and receive a regular, dependable income.

Chris coughs into the microphone, as if he is unsure it is working. Then, he looks up and sweeps the room with his head and smiles at the crowd. His eyes finally rest on Dean Bright, the CEO of Bright Communications.

I sit up taller in the crowd and wait for Chris's eyes to find mine. I can't believe it's actually happening. He's going to propose, after three long years. I'm thirty-three this June. However, I will not be a thirty-three-year old spinster. Nope. Not Joanie Fox!

I wiggle in my seat unable to keep still as Chris croons the usual, "Testing, testing," noises down the mic.

Most of the crowd has spent the evening making good use of the free bar. They mostly stand in suits and skirts looking squiffy and awkward. My bet is that this is lower brow than their usual haunts. Nevertheless, Chris wanted them here and what is important to him is important to me too.

"Doesn't hurt people to know you're serious and committed," Chris had said earlier. It makes sense if you think about it. What better way is there to advertise a dating app than on the back of a strong, healthy relationship?

The crowd are getting bored and one of the younger, more inebriated entrepreneurs starts to wolf-whistle and shout that Chris should 'just get on with it' as we watch Chris wrestle with the mic stand, which is placed at the height for a six footer, and bless Chris he's a few inches shorter than my five-feet-four.

"Well, hello and thank you," he says as though speaking to an applauding crowd. "I want to start by saying Happy New Year. It means the world to me that you've all come so far tonight to celebrate this special evening. I know, when I invented – Sexy Talk Dating – I had a vision, a vision in which hot, beautiful people, like us," Chris sweeps out his hands, palms up, as if hosting a game show, "can meet sexy, like-minded professionals, like us." Chris laughs and thumbs his chest. He looks more nervous than I'm used to seeing him. He takes a sip from his champagne glass and realising that it's empty, he awkwardly tilts his head to ease his nose from the rim.

Chris goes on to tell the audience about his vision for his company, to migrate from the south coast to the city, to buy a huge apartment overlooking the river... I've heard a lot of this over the years, so I tune out a little and down my third shot.

"Why is he taking so long," I moan in Mikey's ear, as

Chris continues to talk about his vision, the inspiration that struck him and how he's never looked back.

It's a quarter to twelve and I don't know how much more the crowd is willing to sustain of this nonsense.

"Get on with it!" someone hollers from the back of the room.

"So, without further ado, Joan will you please come up here?" Chris's voice is a high-pitched squeal as it echoes through the speakers.

I stand with only the slightest need for support, straighten my classy—with a side of cleavage—little black dress, and shimmy up onto the stage. I'm so focused on my task, on getting to the stage with the audience watching, I stumble just a little and misjudge the top step, but I make it in one piece and most importantly, still standing. I hear Mikey wolf-whistle and heckle as he stirs up the crowd. I know both he and Melinda have prepared speeches.

I pause near the middle of the stage and turn to face my soon-to-be betrothed. Chris is now holding a giant bottle of champagne. He's babbling into the mic still. Something about dedication, commitment, and stamina, but the stage lights are making me feel dizzy and a bit sick.

I look around for a single face to focus on, hoping that one constant might make the room stop spinning, but the lights are too bright and the one hundred or so faces are all just blank, cream voids framed by kaleidoscopic hair.

Chris picks up his chatter and I hear the audience chuckle at something he said. I turn to pay attention. His face has a moonlike quality to it; the spotlights highlight the craters of teen acne that he covers with a little of my foundation make-up. His chatter continues, but I can't understand his voice because I'm too worried I might faint or throw up. Or, throw up on the descent into a faint.

The room suddenly stops spinning as Chris's voice holds me to account.

I gulp in preparation.

"So, it is with thanks to the support of this wonderful woman, who I am going to miss like crazy, that I'd like to announce… I'm heading to New York to take—Sexy Talk Dating—to the Big Apple, to send it global!"

I blink a few times and watch Chris smile at the crowd and thrust his fist into the air in triumph.

There's a small round of applause.

My mouth pops open and I stand alone and in shock. A million lights and shiny faces bear witness to my confusion.

My mind stumbles around inside my head, tripping over information, as I try to put together a drunken jigsaw that is damaged and incomplete.

I'm certain Chris didn't just propose because he's still standing on two feet, smiling at me, while he tries to pull the cork from the champagne that is squeezed between his knees.

I'm not engaged.

I'm sure I'm not.

I didn't say yes to anything.

The crowd applauds voraciously as they cheer on the splashing of the astronomically expensive champers. The one Chris insisted I stop and buy on the way here.

He told me that I would want a glass.

I don't just want a glass, I need the bottle and a straw right now.

It dawns on me, as Chris manically chokes the bottle to the delight of the chuckling and jeering crowd, we're not engaged.

We're not engaged AND he's just about to spill MY expensive bottle of champagne.

Anger lights a fuse in my soul and humiliation prepares me for battle.

I have nothing left to lose.

New York?

I lunge towards him.

The cork finally fires, and as if the bottle is a weapon,

there's a boom as it backfires.

Chris stumbles back as the cork shoots out, horizontally across the stage, straight towards me like a heat-seeking missile. It's too fast. I don't have time to leap out of the way or to seek cover and protect myself.

As the missile trajectory fires the cork into my eye, I'm toppled like Jenga. I stagger. One. Two. Three steps. I'm blind from the cork but in my remaining good eye, I see the cake.

As if a near-death experience, time slows and I'm able to admire the cake with its beautiful white lace edging. I silently congratulate Melinda on her good taste as I close in on the table that supports this sweet thing of beauty. Then, unable to brace myself or prevent what I realise is an uncontrollable destiny, I fall and my arms, which have not received the memo, windmill as they futilely try to halt my decent.

I'm floored by the events of this evening.

There is egg on my face, and flour, frosting, and a hint of bitter dark chocolate, if I'm not mistaken. In addition, as if to add sour grapes to the wounds of my ego, I am soaked to my knickers in six-hundred-pound champagne, as Big Ben chimes in the New Year.

Chapter 2

"Joan, let me in." Chris hammers on the door to my ground floor apartment that I now wish was at the top of a skyscraper.

I'm not letting him in.

Last night, after Melinda snatched what was left of the champagne from Chris, she and Mikey took me home and we spent the night drinking while they picked cake frosting from my hair.

My mind is a bit foggy. I can't clearly remember everything that happened after I got home last night, but—lucky for me—there's a technological footprint clearly charting my behaviour.

I have four texts on my phone from Chris apologising. Stating that he now realises that he may have been 'insensitive' dropping the Big Apple bomb on the stage and that he understands how much I will miss him while he is away. He has even forgiven me for hitting him with the mic stand.

My replies were brief. The first reads: You fucking fuck! The rest are even worse.

Then there was the video Mikey emailed me: Me trying

to climb through the foyer window of my building and landing on my head.

"Please, babe. Take the dead bolt off and let me in. Let's talk about this," he calls through the door.

If I were not one hundred percent certain standing up would unleash a tsunami of vomit, I would so get up, take the styling wand from the dresser next to my bed, and go jam it into his eye.

Oh my God, my eye!

I cup the socket of my eye as a flashback involving a cork missile replays in my head. Heat flushes my cheeks and I leap to my feet to look at my face in the mirror above my dresser.

My eye is swollen and almost shut. Red and purplish bruising marks the spot where the cork unapologetically punched me in my face.

I'm awash with humiliation and anger at Chris. My hands ball at my sides and I stomp to the door. I fling it open, not caring that I'm only wearing last night's black lace underwear that I chose in readiness to start our engagement with a bang.

Now, well now, I'm ready to lose the last of my dignity and scream at Chris to get his things and go, and never dare to return.

With the door wide open, my hands meet my hips in defiance. However, the doorway is empty. I wonder if I imagined Chris's ramblings. I step outside of the door to check, my fists still curled into hammers ready to attack. My anger is a bomb ready for detonation. I glare up the hallway, pissed at his retreat.

"Chris?" I angrily yell to the empty corridor that's lined by the eight red doors that match mine.

Realising that he has already left, I turn to head back inside my apartment when I feel a tap on my shoulder.

"Hi, neighbour. Is this yours...?" A gravelly, male voice that I do not recognise purrs.

I swivel my body and gawk up at the dark haired,

chiselled face towering at least a foot above my own. He's dressed in dark jeans and a fitted shirt and, fuck me, if that isn't the sexiest damned stubble and just-been-screwed hair I've ever seen.

My mouth swings open, unprepared for this vision of hotness. His mouth opens too.

Suddenly, I feel self-conscious and naked.

Shit – I'm naked!

Bolstered by my embarrassment, anger spits like lava from my pores and I aim my glare in a new direction.

"Can I help you? What? You never seen a woman in her underwear in a hallway before?"

I don't wait for his answer. I take three steps and storm into my apartment. I'm about to slam my door in his ungrateful, square-jawed, too-handsome face when he jars the door with his foot and pushes his index finger forward into the gap. Dangled from his finger is one lowly black, sling-backed shoe. I recognise it from the Christmas sale in Topshop. A shoe that deserves the look of spite I'm piercing it with now because I know that traitorous bitch pinched my toes and offered zero support during my time of need.

His dark eyes demand my attention. I stare up at them, marvelling in the arch of his brow and decide I must deny all knowledge of the shoe.

"Actually, I found this in the foyer and I wondered if it was yours?" His mouth curves up into a grin.

"No. Nothing to do with me!" I lie as my mind wanders back to the incriminating video Mikey sent me this morning.

The main door to our building had stuck. It's not the first time I've had to climb through the window of the foyer. Chris used to push me up to climb through it regularly.

I die a little inside at the thought that this mountain of a man may have witnessed my second humiliation of the night. I dismiss the thought. My neighbour looks like he is only just coming home, probably from an all-night shag-fest.

I fan myself a little as heat rises within me. He interrupts my indecent thoughts.

"Really? I wondered if the cold had made the door stick. You're the only neighbour I've noticed who might wear such a shoe, and I thought I'd best return it, Cinders." His tone is cocky. He damn well knows it's my shoe and, even though I'm very cross with it right now, I have a matching one in my apartment that will be sad and lonely without it. Therefore, I do what any shoe loving embarrassed fool would do, I snatch the shoe with my left hand and slam the door with my right.

I hear a shocked intake of breath and lean up to watch him swipe his dark hair across his head from the safety of the peephole. He shakes his head and calls to me from the other side of my door.

"Very mature, number four," he says, pursing his swollen lips in judgment.

"Yeah, well it's a little late in life for you to be doing the walk of shame, number two!"

"It's number six, actually, Four," he calls back.

"Yeah, well Six, your fly is undone." It is a cheap shot, I know. Nonetheless, when he lifts his shirt to reveal his tight, tanned abs as he checks his crotch, the reward is priceless.

He grins upwards, his eyes dark in their gaze and a naughty expression closes in on the peephole. "You enjoy a peep show, huh, Four? Duly-noted." Six taps his nose and he cockily heads to the door next to mine.

My cheeks are on fire as I clutch my shoe to my chest, then realising it has frosting caked to its heel, I throw that traitorous bitch on the floor and head back to bed. It may be New Year's Day, a time for new beginnings and all that crap, but I am going to hug my pillow. I grab a bowl from the kitchen as I pass, just in case I need to throw up.

This year can kiss my ass.

***

"Ooh. That looks nasty. You sure you don't have a concussion?" Melinda asks as she passes me the gravy boat.

"Why does Joanie have a boo-boo?" Tegan rubs her own eye as she asks me about my bruise.

"Joanie just needs to figure out how to walk properly in her shoes and how to dodge stray missiles. Eat up your greens," Melinda instructs her seven-year-old daughter.

"Joanie may not have dodged the cork, but she definitely dodged a bullet." Mikey laughs as he pushes Melinda's lumpy mashed potatoes around the plate.

It's New Year's Day and Melinda has gone all out to cook a nice dinner for me, Mikey and her four adorable kids. Melinda's husband, who works in banking, was called away on business right after Christmas lunch. To be honest, I'm a bit confused as to what the emergency might have been, but because Mikey and I both know this fact won't have escaped Melinda, we don't bring up his absence.

We help Melinda bathe and put the kids to bed, and then we settle back on the settee with a glass of wine. It doesn't take long before Mikey raises my recent disaster.

"So, have you seen Cautious Chris yet?" Mikey sniggers.

I explain the disaster that was this morning, leaving out my encounter with Six. If they knew about that, there would be a whole lot more teasing.

"Shouldn't I be devastated?" I ask them. "He announces that he's going to New York for six months, and now that I've processed it, I feel relieved. How can I be disappointed that he didn't propose, yet relieved that I don't have to spend another six months with him? It's as if I've been desperately clinging to a relationship that's doomed because I've been convinced it's my last shot at happiness."

I drink more wine, not because it helps with my confusion, clearly it doesn't, but because I'm not sure I'm ready to face the reality of my confession. However, reality is a sneaky bitch and my realisation causes me to blurt, "I'm old and past it, and I'm terrified that if I don't settle down soon I'll be a miserable old spinster right up until I die, old, and wrinkly, and old, and alone." I dramatically throw my hands in the air, spilling some wine on my jeans, emphasising my point.

Mikey thinks this is hilarious and spits a little of his wine out to prove it.

"You're not that old and you're gorgeous. Chris wasn't the only person to see that and he won't be the last. Come-on Joanie, Chris was a calamity. He's done you a favour, and if you don't meet anyone, you can always rely on me. I'll make sure your cats get re-homed when you die."

"I don't have any cats," I tell him, pointing my finger.

"Not yet you don't. But, you'll probably want to get some if you're to look the part."

"Mikey, I'm only six months older than you!" I say incredulously. "Where's your happily ever after, huh?"

"I get laid five times a week, sweetie. It's not me we need to be worried about."

Melinda casts a measuring glance at both of us.

"I'm not worried. At least I wasn't until you started talking about cats. Oh my God, you think that don't you? You think I'll die alone."

The wine has worked its evil magic and I start to feel loose-tongued and emotional.

"Both of you pack it in," Melinda says sternly, as if she is talking to her kids. "The way I see it, you should have dumped Chris way back. Like when he bought you that awful watch." I glance down at the Chinese lettering on the clock face that is always a beat behind. "In fact, Joanie, you should have dumped him way before that. Like when you had your tonsils out and he went skiing with his mates instead of taking care of you. You've been hanging onto the wrong guy, sweetie, and you are worth so much more. Have you even officially broken up with him yet?" Melinda asks.

I look sheepishly at the cheap watch that is suddenly burning a rash on my wrist. I tug and pull at it and then shove it in the pocket of my jeans.

"What? So, everyone knew Chris was wrong for me, apart from me?" Why am I only just coming to this conclusion when in fact he has been a self-centred dick for a long time? I shake my head. I'm so stupid.

"Ha! You didn't dump him yet. Joanie, what the fuck..." Mikey finds this hilarious.

"I haven't seen him yet," I say in my defence. It's the best excuse I have, but even as the words leave my mouth, I know the real reason. "I don't want to be alone again," I admit.

Mikey's arm snakes around my waist, and Melinda is out of her seat and cradling my head as she shushes my sobs.

"I don't even know how to date. These days it's all plenty of frogs and I don't want to kiss any more toads. I'll tell him tomorrow," I say, nodding my head, my mind made up. "There's plenty more frogs to kiss, right?"

"Honey, there's plenty of fucking men out there. I'll even let you have the straight ones..." Mikey tells me.

"Joanie. Before Chris, you spent all your time picking faults in guys, looking for reasons not to date them: their shoes were too square, their hair was too short, their jeans were too baggy…"

"Ooh. What about the one whose ears were too pointy," Mikey interrupts Melinda with a giggle and she nods.

"You found Chris. He looked good enough on the outside, your parents loved him, and that was it. You settled," Melinda explains, and I find myself nodding. "You're too picky. You need to let yourself go and just live in the moment. What will be will be."

"Um, Melinda, I hate to tell you this, but you are the most tightly-strung woman I know. Where on earth does this new mantra come from?" I ask.

"Never you mind. I'm right," Melinda replies, reverting back to the Melinda I'm most familiar with. "You just need to get back out there and you'll find 'the one' in no time."

"Thank you." I sob and snot into Mikey's pink Armani shirt. When he notices, he holds me at arms length and announces, "Fuck it. Let's get you shit-faced!"

***

After quite a bit more wine, mostly shared between Mikey and I, I pay a visit to the little girl's room and announce that I'm going to walk home. Melinda and Mikey are in fits of laughter about something, and I'm glad the mood has exponentially lightened since my mini breakdown. Melinda wants to order me a taxi, but I insist that the walk will do me good; it's only a five-minute walk, anyway.

As I approach my 1920s, Art Deco style apartment block, I'm relieved to see the foyer light has been left on. The lighting is limited up our driveway, which can make the stiff lock of the front door even more difficult to navigate.

Then I notice something unusual.

A dark silhouette paces back and forth, beneath the blinking strip light. I am about to slow down, to assess whether it is an axe murderer or a neighbour, when the figure turns and glares right at me.

I'm too close to the entrance to hide, so I casually proceed with caution. As I near, the door flings open and Chris grabs me by the arms and yanks me inside. The action causes me to stumble.

"Where the hell have you been? I came by earlier and I've been phoning you. Why haven't you been answering?"

Chris yells.

I shake him off, and being a little drunk, I yell, "Get your hands off me. Don't you dare ever touch me again! We are through. Do you hear me? Through." I swing my arms back so he can't reach my hands.

"I'm sorry Joan. I wanted to tell you earlier, but I was waiting to hear about my Visa and I was worried you would jinx everything. We can make it work. I know we can." Chris starts moving towards me again. With every step he takes forward I take two back.

Suddenly he repulses me and I can't see anything that's attractive about him.

Then I notice his suitcase on the floor behind him. "Did you go into my apartment?" I yell, furious at the intrusion.

"I needed my stuff. My laptop and my passport. I fly to New York tomorrow. I wanted to say goodbye."

"That's it," I spit. The alcohol is making me giddy, but I don't care. The thought of him in my space makes me want to hurt him.

"Get out!"

"You're upset. I understand now, I should have told you. Baby, I'll give you some time to get used to the idea and I'll call you. You'll see it was worth it."

He walks towards me and holds out his lips as if to kiss me goodbye. I give him a two handed shove. This is my closure and Chris deserves my wrathful beating. I'm amazed he still doesn't even seem aware of how appallingly he has treated me.

"Don't call me and don't message me. I hope your dick falls off!"

The word dick echoes through the hallway as if to taunt me. My hands are shaking and I have to clench to hold them still.

I'm about to continue to lash him with my anger when I'm interrupted by a gruff, masculine voice. "Is everything okay? Four, are you all right? I heard the yelling all the way from my apartment."

I follow the voice along the carpeted foyer all the way to Six, who only has a white bath towel wrapped around his waist. Droplets of water fall from his hair and roll over his pectoral muscles. They continue a path down his concrete abs pooling in his tiny circular navel.

Six clears his throat, and my eyes shoot to his. At his raised eyebrow, I close my mouth, and then look back at Chris, whose mouth is also open.

"Of course, I'm fine. He was just going." I shove my thumb in Chris's direction and glare from him to the door.

"You heard the lady." Six cocks his head towards the door, then pulls his towel a little tighter.

Chris raises his hands in defeat and makes a show of pulling the handle of his wheeled suitcase up, to show his intent to leave.

As Chris reluctantly walks out of the door, he turns to tell me, "I'll call you." The door swings closed behind him and I sigh in relief and turn my attention back to Six. The draft from the door's closure causes Six's near black hair to swing back and drip more water down his body.

I swallow hard and, unsure what to say or where to look without embarrassing myself further, I attempt to glide down the corridor with a sassy little butt swing. However, because I already drank the best part of two bottles of wine, my glide turns into a petulant stomp and the stupid kitten heel of my boot does not allow me to glide. No, it has other ideas. It latches on the tasselled rug, which behaves like an octopus, tangling around my feet. Before I'm able to right my balance, I fall face first, straight towards Six and his moist, poster-perfect body.

My arms flail around as I attempt to reverse my trajectory, and I yelp as I fall in slow motion towards the floor. The yelp echoes through the corridor, alerting anyone who may not be aware that I'm making a complete fool of myself, that they should stop what they are doing to come watch this ridiculous debacle.

Six is alert and leaps into action. He swoops and bends to catch me.

My arms launch out like the wheels of a jet plane in order to save myself, just in case his thick strong arms aren't up to the job. I latch hold of the first thing my hands can get purchase on. Not the heavy bookcase or the tub chair next to the entrance to our corridor, no, because they might actually break my fall. Instead, I grab onto what might possibly be the worst thing in the world to grab when falling.

The towel.

Not just any towel.

THE towel.

The towel that is sheltering his groin, to be precise.

My right hand clings, as though it is my lifeline, onto what I am certain is a large semi erect penis, covered in one-hundred-percent Egyptian cotton towelling.

The penis is robust and between it and his strong arms, they prevent my face from kissing the floor.

Six lifts me higher, so that my eyes meet his dark, almost navy blue, glittering lakes. He smiles a sexy lopsided grin and my skin, lit by desire, heats into a fast boil.

Six's features crinkle a little and he gives me a measured, concerned look. Then he says, "It's okay, Four. You're safe. You can let go of my penis now, if you want to, that is."

Six gives me the sexiest grin I have ever seen this close and in person, and then he winks.

He actually winks.

I do what any normal, lucid, self-conscious woman would do under the circumstances. As if it is suddenly on fire, I drop the penis and run like hell to the safety of my apartment.

Chapter 3

Before I go to work in the morning, I check the peephole to make sure the hallway is clear and Six is not around. I give myself eye strain glaring, and I listen for any signs of movement in the hallway outside. As I do this, thoughts of last night invade my mind.

After penis-gate, once I was safely in my flat, I spent what was left of the evening giving myself an ear bashing about what just happened. It's as I told Melinda, when I called her to offload, who has a penis that large? It is obscene, glutinous. It wouldn't even fit. As soon as I had made that statement, I had started to wonder about all the ways that it might fit, and then I really couldn't sleep.

This morning, I'm tired, a little hung-over and a lot horny. A part of my problem was my overactive imagination competing with my under-sexed body. Chris and I hadn't had sex for months; he was just too busy or tired.

One grip of a massive penis and now suddenly I've become Wanton Wilma.

I smack my head with my palm; I just need to get some. Then, maybe I can get Six, I mean sex, out of my head.

I hear footsteps and hold my breath as Six walks within sight of my peephole. Paranoid thoughts wage a war against any rational thinking, and I wonder if he can somehow see me spying on him from behind my door.

I suddenly feel like some kind of naked peeping Tom. Not that I'm actually naked, but suddenly my red raincoat feels lewd and sinister. I quickly hang it back on the hook and swap it for a green Parker coat, and I congratulate myself for avoiding Six. Just a few more minutes and I should be able to leave for work.

When I return to check the peephole, Six has stopped right outside my door to tie his shoe. He dons a sexy little grin that turns the corner of his mouth up. He then slowly stands, looks right at me through my peephole and walks away, as if he didn't just eye fuck me through a door.

Big dick Six walks with a cocky swagger. Maybe his giant penis makes him walk this way, all confident and smooth. I channel my desire into distaste.

Yuk!

Six needs to stop being such a smug bastard. Swaggering past my hole as if he owns it, who does he think he is?

I strain my neck, trying to get a better angle of him walking away. For a moment, I get a good view of his muscular butt as he continues up the hall and out of view. Perhaps someone ought to buy him a wheelbarrow for his giant cock in case he throws his back out.

With Six safely out of view, I rub the tension in my neck and grab my bag and keys from the console table next to the door. I'm just about to leave when an important thought pops into my head. From now on, I can't open the door without first checking if he is in the corridor. I will need to learn his routine if I am to continue to avoid that hugely hung bastard.

Because I am paranoid and I can't trust myself not to accidentally walk out to the hallway without checking, I go to the kitchen and pull a notepad from the drawer. I tear out a sheet and scribble on it: Look for sex. Then, because I always check my work, I cross out sex and change the word to Six.

Look for ~~sex~~ Six.

I add three exclamation marks to highlight the importance of looking for Six and then, satisfied I have done all I can do to avoid Six, I pin the note to the inside of my door. After a reasonable amount of time, I walk out of my door and turn left towards the foyer, walking confidently in the direction of the car park.

The corridor lacks its usual musty smell. It smells like Six. His rugged, earthy cologne is uplifting against the noxious scent of One's day old curry and Two's elderly poodle. I inhale deeply just to be sure I recognise the smell for future reference. However, as I'm nearing the end of the corridor, the scent sharpens and Six suddenly turns the corner.

I can't trust myself to say anything coherent to him, not at this ungodly hour, so I inhale him once more and continue, intending to walk past him.

He stands there, as if expecting me to stop and talk to him some more.

After penis-gate!

His hair looks lighter today, now that it's not oozing water down his hard, broad shoulders. It's dishevelled, yanked in all directions, and I have a strong urge to run my hand through his hair and give it a little tug of my own, just to see if it really feels as soft as it looks. Instead, I ball my hands in the pockets of my Parker. Intending to rush past him, muttering something about being in a hurry, I sprint towards my car.

He sidesteps in an attempt to move out of my way, but I already sidestepped him first. In my haste to avoid him, I bump into his rock hard chest. Six-foot-something manliness crashes against me.

Six brazenly grabs hold of my hands to stop me from

falling backwards onto the corduroy carpet. My pulse gallops against his rough hands, and I'm rendered completely speechless as he stands opposite me. Up close, he smells even better; I inhale a little deeper. My nostrils flare as I quickly try to expel his scent from inside of me.

He grins with a knowing smile that he's gotten beneath my skin. His navy blue eyes, that match his suit, are thorough in their assessment of me.

I try to look away, but my traitorous gaze is now trained on his groin, which today is sheathed in an expensive looking, tight trouser. I forcibly drag my eyes away and instead train them on the area just ahead of Six and the foyer beyond.

"Good morning, Four. I'm glad I've run into you. I forgot my wallet, was just running back to get it, coincidence seeing you out here at this hour." He smiles. His teeth are white and gleam like freshly fallen snow. "After you ran off last night, I wanted to check on you, to see if that man last night was bothering you? Then you seemed a little flushed, so I thought I would wait until today. Is he the reason your face is bruised?" Six stands rigid and his face is serious as he inspects my eye.

I gaze up at him. This close to him, I can see the turquoise flecks in his dark eyes. A light crinkling to the skin around them marks his concern. It's then I realise that Six thinks I'm might be some kind of battered wife. I try to tell him, to set the record straight, but the words leave my mouth in a gurgled mess, as if my communication skills have leapt back by three decades. "No, he didn't… Well, it was a misfire, you see. A missile badly let off, he didn't mean to… He didn't hit me, if that's what you're wondering. I'm single actually."

Six smiles and replies, "So, you're okay?" He steps back as he lets go of my hands. "That's good." He nods.

I correct myself when I notice that, as his scent retreats, I'm leaning forward. My eyes trail down his body, distracting me. His jacket is open and his shirt is pure white with the slightest sheen. I stop myself gawking at the silhouette of his chest. However, when I attempt to look away, my eyes lock on his groin again. My tongue moistens my lips, and an alarming fact smacks me upside the head.

It's official. I am a pervert.

"Yes, yes, Six. I'm fine," I mumble, shaking my head to clear my dirty thoughts, and I begin walking away.

Six grabs my wrist loosely and I freeze in place, half in the corridor, half in the foyer. I don't dare turn back and meet his gaze for fear of what my body might do.

"You know, Four. If you ever need anything, anything at all, I'm right next door. You don't have to keep running off. We could be friends you and I."

The mint on his breath is a tickle on my neck and I can't help turn to him. He really is a thing of beauty, so much so I actually feel my knees weaken.

"You know, Six, maybe I'd like that," I reply honestly. So long as I can stop humiliating myself in front of him, Six may be just the scratch to my itch. My mouth turns up in a smile and I decide this is just what I need, a little practice at the art of flirting, a little fun. Six smiles back mischievously; his hair flops a little over his eye as his head turns to an oncoming voice.

"There you are. I was about to run after you, you forgot your wallet..."

Barbie, A.K.A. Big-Tits-Twenty, my neighbour, the one Chris shagged, is walking towards us, all naked legs and dishevelled hair. She also hosts the quarterly owners' meetings held in the Dancing Deer, which is a bar down the road. Her long blonde hair sways in time with her silicone breasts, beating her bare feet to us by a long shot. She's dressed in a belted oversized shirt. Six's shirt, I'd bet.

Six drops my wrist and takes a step towards Twenty. She purrs as she hands him his wallet and rubs up against him like a cat in heat, marking her territory. She eyes me cautiously while she waits for Six to speak.

Six smiles pleasantly at us both in turn.

"Thanks, Barb, you're a lifesaver. You ladies have a great day," he says and walks away toward the foyer and out of our line of sight. Big-Tits-Twenty and I stare after him, our mouths more than a little agape.

"I... got to go," we say in unison and head in our separate directions.

I stomp to my car and decide two important things. One, I still hate Big-Tits-Twenty, and two, my sense of smell cannot be trusted for risk-assessing the corridor, and I make a mental note to buy some deodorisers on my way home from work.

***

I spend the day at work calming myself, which is much easier to do beyond the reach of Six's pheromones. However, as soon as work is finished and I pull the car up outside our building, I'm a bag of nerves again. I manage to navigate the car park like a secret agent, hiding in the shadows and sticking to the grass, which is quieter to walk on. The door to the foyer sticks, as usual. I eye the window I sometimes need to climb through because apparently I'm the only person in the building who has any difficulty with the stiffness of the lock, and for that reason the maintenance company refuses to fix it.

After a few waggles of my key and a shoulder bump to the door, I'm in the foyer and racing to my apartment, mentally patting my skills on the proverbial back. My nerves really kick in when I get to our corridor. However, it's clear of Six, and I have my key ready, so I'm able to shoot through the door, making it within the safety zone in record time.

Phew. I breathe a sigh of relief and relax.

My phone rings from my bag and makes me jump. I can see from the call display that it's Melinda, checking up on me no doubt. She immediately asks why I'm so jumpy and I explain to her about this morning's situation, following Penis-gate and my subsequent anxiety around him.

"It's no good. I'm just going to have to sell up and buy somewhere new," I tell her, while moving around the kitchen, filling and switching on the kettle.

"He can't be that bad," Melinda says.

"He is, he really is," I insist, but she just doesn't get it. Probably because I don't tell her how good-looking he is, so she doesn't take me seriously and changes the subject on my neurotic mumblings.

"How's your eye? Did you try the cover-up I told you about?"

It's dark outside so I check out my reflection in the kitchen window. "My eye looks less swollen. It's all the way open now, so it's almost better. I bought some concealer anyway, so I'll give it a try tomorrow."

"Good. I was thinking, when you look a little more runway model than road-kill victim, we need to get you back out there. I've written a list, I hope you don't mind, of some of the singles who might be good matches. This time, we're not going to leave it to that sick son-of-a-bitch fate. We'll do our research, plan better, and then we can secure a better outcome. I was thinking, a little older this time, someone who already knows what he wants. Someone ambitious, but not like Chris, and he should definitely be a homeowner."

I hear Mikey in the background wetting himself with laughter.

"I think a homeowner will be more interested in me than Joanie," Mikey hollers.

"I didn't know Mikey was staying with you again," I say, changing the subject. The last thing I need is Melinda on a matchmaking mission.

"He is. He and Ted had a big fight, tell you later," she whispers.

"So, since you're worried you're getting on a bit, and there's no time to waste, I've made a spreadsheet of every single guy we know. I also went through Mikey's address book of straights, and Steve's address book too. We need numbers. It's no good putting all your eggs in one basket. You've got to kiss a lot of frogs. Do it a lot of times. Steve and I had sex twice a day for three months before Ed was conceived. Everything takes more time and effort the older you get."

"Mel, please stop with the matchmaking. It's only been two days since I got out from a long-term relationship. I need time."

"Nonsense. You need numbers."

I have visions of Melinda pushing spectacles up her nose, closer to her eyes, as she examines her spreadsheet.

"She got me too, Joanie. We're fucked. Only she reckons I've got too many numbers, so with me it's the opposite."

Melinda clarifies, "Mikey's already screwed his way around town. Therefore, we're going with quality not quantity, no more seedy nightclubs and Internet hook-ups. For Mikey it's all about the serious, dedicated homosexuals looking for life partners. I'll have you two settled down before Ed's out of nappies. We start potty training next week. So, both of you, stock up on condoms and for God's sake Joanie, put on that concealer and make sure you look at the email I sent you. I want a short list of ten names by the end of the week."

"Ten?" I ask, humouring her.

"Yes, ten. Statistically speaking, if you date ten guys, in ten days, at least one will be a keeper. Left to you, you'll be procrastinating over what shoes they're wearing and worrying whether your mother will like them. This way we cut out the BS and skip straight to the good part."

I gulp.

Ten guys, ten dates.

"Have you lost your mind? This isn't Joanie does Jamaica. What are you doing to Mikey? His punishment had better be worse," I threaten.

"Oh it is, J. Next week is my week off, she's booked me onto intense cookery one-oh-one. It's going to be fucking torture."

"What if we decide we won't do it?" I ask, knowing she can't enforce this shit.

"I'm cutting you both off. I'm not listening to anymore whining about Crappy Chris, Joanie, and Mikey, I won't listen to a single word about Ted the Tosser, either. You'll both be on your own. It's my way or the highway. If I fail, which of course I won't, I won't ever cast a disparaging glance at either one of you, ever again. Deal?"

"Deal," Mikey and I both begrudgingly say in unison.

Chapter 4

After a long hot bubble bath, I pick up my ageing laptop and scan through the spreadsheet that Melinda sent me. She's put in a lot of effort and it's plain to see that she is indeed playing the numbers game. It's got forty-two 'options' and a sidebar of colour-coded 'additional information.' My eyes widen at the list of interests, backgrounds, whether they have kids, were married previously, and what car they drive. She's even scored them in terms of suitability and sustainability. Melinda is meticulous if not a little mental.

After a full hour of perusing my options and being unable to decide, I slam my laptop shut and call Mikey. "This is ridiculous. I'm not shopping for a mortgage. Number eighteen is a two-star suitability and five-star sustainability! What the hell does that even mean? Well, we're not doing it, Mikey. I'm putting my foot down."

Mikey interrupts. "Shh, J. It's okay. We're going to humour her," he whispers down the line, so I assume he's still over at Melinda's place. "There's something you don't know. I only found out because I picked up the landline phone earlier by mistake. Steve was calling—asking to come home. He's not working away; she threw him out. He didn't say what he did, but it must be bad. She keeps going quiet and yesterday—and you tell no one about this—she hugged me and told me that, even though it's hard sometimes, I have to believe in true love. She's behaving really strangely. The last time I broke up with Ted, she punched me and told me to get back out there. So, you see, we shut up and put up with it because it's keeping her mind off the separation, and she's obviously not ready to tell us yet. We do whatever she needs. Agreed?"

I swallow down my sadness. Melinda and Steve got married on the same day that Brad married Jen. I was sure when Brad knocked up Angie that it would have no bearing on Melinda and Steve; they were as solid as a brick. Turns out, maybe I should have been concerned.

"Mikey," I whisper.

"Yeah?"

"You know Angie left Brad?"

"Yeah, I do."

"Do you think they'll get back together?"

"I don't know, J." Mikey sighs. "It'll be all right, though. There's always Kim and Kanye."

I gulp down a lump. I feel like my own parents just broke up.

"So we do as Melinda says?" I ask.

"Yeah, until she's ready to tell us."

"Okay." I pull a tissue from the box on the coffee table. "Mikey, can you choose my numbers? I don't think I can."

"Already did, babe," he replies. "Joanie, I start cookery lessons this week. She thinks it'll be good for me. You will eat my shit, won't you?"

"Of course, Mikey, we're in this together."

We say goodbye and I put down my phone, ready to have a good blub. It's the end of an era, Steve and Melinda are like surrogate parents to Mikey and me; always inviting us over, Steve checking the oil in my car, and Melinda sending us home with food parcels. Knowing that Melinda is sad and alone right now upsets me more than when my parents told me they were retiring abroad. If she needs me to date ten random men, in ten damned days to take her mind off things, then that's what I'll do.

***

I wake suddenly with a jolt. I'm lying on my back. The sheets are a sweaty mess around me, and no matter how hard I try to sink back into the abyss, sleep eludes me like Santa in June.

Right before bed, I made the mistake of stalking Chris on social media and now I'm awash with self-pity. Chris changed his profile picture. It's now a selfie of him standing in front of the Statue of Liberty clutching a six-foot blonde; at least she looks about that height next to shorter-than-average Chris.

I hear the hinges of the foyer door groan as they are forced into action. The neon light of my alarm clock display informs me that it's two-forty-five a.m. and I wonder who is coming home this late on a Tuesday evening. With my interest piqued, I rush to spy through the peephole, just in case it's a burglar.

It isn't a burglar.

No, it's Six. Like a thief in the night, he stumbles toward my door. He turns and stops opposite the hole, peering in, as if it's a two-way mirror. My heart beats like a drum and I hold my breath, frightened of making the slightest noise.

Six is wearing a dark V-neck T-shirt and casual slim jeans. He runs his hands through his floppy hair. Like silk, it slides back into place. He peers closer to my peephole.

It's as if he can actually see me.

Even though it's probably wasted, I give him my best stink eye and stare him out through the hole. Yes, Six, I am annoyed with you for stumbling in at this ungodly hour and making noises like you are trying to provoke a response from me.

My knees tremble from the draft that whooshes under the door and up my short Princess Fiona bed shirt.

Six steps back and grins. He sways his hips and starts to bellow an awful rendition of Nelly's, Hot In Here.

His voice lacks its normal gravelly smoothness. He stumbles as he performs in the corridor, right in front of my door. It's then that I detect faint, spicy and smoky tones in the air. I lower my body to sniff the draft under the door.

Six has whisky breath.

The scent, on top of his usual sweet, woody smell makes my skin sensitise and goose bump. My mouth waters and I crave a taste of his whisky. He's drunk, but more importantly, he starts to take off his shirt.

"It's getting hot in here, I'm taking off my clothes..." When he forgets the words, he just mumbles, "Duh, duh, duh..."

My eyes widen with a pop. He really does take off his shirt. He flings it on the floor and a gasp leaves my mouth. His shoulders are broad and strong, as if they could carry boulders or skinny little dark haired women with ease.

"Four, are you there?"

Six peers closer. His pupils are huge black, circular discs. His gaze is so intense I lean forward, bumping my head on the cold wood of the door. Shit! I close my eyes to stop from feeling dizzy but leave my head on the door to anchor me.

"Four, I know you're there," he sings. "Do you have any special requests?"

I stay silent. There's no way he can be certain I'm here.

"Four..." He sings, louder. "Open up or I'll blow your house down..."

I open my eyes, needing to see him. Even drunk, he looks like a cool glass of water here to put out my fire.

"Hey, J. I'm not sure how you thought you were going to get home without your keys." There's a jangle, and I glance around the peripheral of my spy hole. It's Big-Tits-Twenty. I recognise her sickly, purring voice, even though I can't quite see her yet. She sounds like a room full of tortured cats.

My teeth grind on themselves. What does J mean? John, Jacob, Jack? Why does she get to know his name?

"Hey, my saviour." Six turns away from my door to face her.

"How much did you drink? That's not even your door, silly." She giggles. It sounds like someone stepped on her tail. "Here, let me help you." Twenty comes into view, and I see her link her arm around Six's waist and pull him away from me, along the corridor to his apartment next door.

Their voices fade. I go into my bedroom. I know the layout of the flat next door. It's a mirror image of my own. I held the key for the agent while it was on the market, but I never met Six. The agent just said it was an overseas investor. I thought its new purpose would be short holiday lets. An apartment upstairs has a similar use.

I sit on my bed and rest my weary head above my headboard, against the wall.

"Whoa hold up. That's it, on the bed..." Twenty's laugh is like a hyena's mating call.

My stomach flips in on itself. I lie down and pull my pillow over my head to try and distract myself from their drunken sounds. The walls are paper-thin. It makes me wonder how much sound proofing costs. I take my head out from under my pillow and grab my phone off the nightstand to check. I'm annoyed to see that it's very expensive. Perhaps I should invoice Six.

There's a laughing hyena in the apartment next door. Twenty's harrumphs echo through the wall. My blood races at a quickened pace. It's then that Six's headboard knocks against my wall.

They must be trying to annoy me.

I bolt upright, about to fist my hand on the wall and shout at them to shuddup! But instead, I sit on my hands. I can't do that. They would know that I could hear them. That I'm listening. I'm too embarrassed; I wouldn't be able to look either of them in the eye ever again. They would make jokes to each other that I am a jealous prude.

My mouth falls open.

I have sex envy.

It's been too long.

I sigh, grab my phone, duvet, and pillow and get up to go into the lounge. I'll sleep on the sofa tonight.

I lay back and try to get comfortable. Even though I can't be certain they are having sex, it's suddenly gone quiet over there and my mind races, imaging what Six is like in bed.

I imagine myself under his heavy weight. His sizeable expanse pressing down on me, delicious friction creating a frenzy. A low ache forms in my belly and heat pools in long frozen-over places. I'm so tempted to bring myself some light relief, but I can't allow myself to. Not with her next door with him, it would feel voyeuristic and tainted.

I fetch my headphones and put them on, switching the volume up loud on my playlist.

I can't get Nelly's song out of my head.

***

After the worst night's sleep, I wake before my alarm detonates, with a crook in my neck and an aching deep in my belly. I stand up and stretch out my thoroughly aching, and not in a good way, muscles. When it all went quiet over at Six's apartment, my hands once again wandered of their own accord, aiming to get some much needed relief. I was embarrassingly turned on. The noises from the apartment next door had me crossing my legs and singing the alphabet for distraction.

Knowing the length and girth of his instrument only

made matters worse. The images were too vivid. But, no matter how much I wanted relief, it wouldn't come! I was my own worst enemy. Needing but not getting, wanting but not having.

A thought terrified me. How could I satisfy a new partner if I couldn't even satisfy myself?

In the end, I angrily log onto the shopping sites and search some reviews on equipment to aide my dilemma. Finally, I settle on the aptly named Come-Hard-6000. It was sleek and black and came with a six-year warranty and a pleasure guarantee—or your money back.

The alarm on my smart phone starts to tinkle, so I switch it off and walk into the kitchen. I begin my normal morning routine by taking out some bread to toast and switch on the kettle to boil.

It's still dark outside, but I can hear the wind beating against the tall oaks in the expansive garden of our building. I catch sight of my reflection in the window and notice the Christmas excess is taking its toll on my usually thinner physique. I pinch at the start of a muffin top and, already feeling tired and unattractive, I pop the bread out of the machine and fling it in the bin. I'll start a January health kick. I'll take up jogging, or yoga. I'll learn the downward dog and get all bendy and flexible. Maybe Twenty will see me all lithe and bendy and she'll be jealous of my B cups and demand that her G cups be removed at once.

I unpeel a brown, limp banana and hear the creak of a door opening. I run to my peephole to spy.

I recognise Twenty's gnarly hushed voice echoing in the hallway, even though she's not in my eye line. Maybe I need to shop for a more comprehensive peephole, for added security. Something that better scopes out the whole hallway. Perhaps we should have CCTV. I could get one of those apps so I can view it from anywhere. Crime is on the up, after all.

After an age of whispering, Twenty walks past my door

on her way to the foyer, probably to take the stairs up to her apartment. She fluffs her yellow hair as she walks past, like she just walked out of a salon. She blazingly does the walk of shame in only a shirt. His shirt. Her feet are bare.

I think back to last week and Two's incontinent dog as she walks over a dark patch on the carpet. My grin high-fives my ears.

I back away from the door and start the shower, deciding that today I'll switch on some music while I ready myself for work. It should be loud on a thundery day like today, rock music is probably best.

My phone beeps a new tone, one I don't recognise. Melinda's voice, "Warning, dating emergency; dating emergency. You have two minutes to respond to this message or you will die a lonely spinster." I then hear Mikey in the background call out, "With one hundred cats!"

I remember them, the last time I was at Melinda's house, creasing up after I left the bathroom to head home, not getting their private joke. Now I know. They changed my text message alert.

When I open the message, it simply reads—Date tonight. 5 p.m. at the Brit. He'll be wearing a hat.

I instantly dial her back.

"Hello, Joanie, your dating fairy godmother here," Melinda, sings into my ear.

"Hi." I keep my voice level and compose my thoughts. "So, I saw your message." I wait with baited breath for her to spin me some yarn about how wonderful Mr. X is.

"Good. You'll see from the report I emailed you that he is a four out of five in suitability, three out of five in sustainability but he might surprise us on that front. The jury's out until you actually go on the date. No, Teeg, don't put sugar on the Chocó pops; they're full of the stuff as it is... Look Joanie, I'm sorry, I've got to get the kids to school, and I'm meeting with a lawyer, and... call me later, promise?"

I think back to my earlier conversation with Mikey. A lawyer must mean that the split is serious. My throat closes in on itself. She hasn't talked this through with me. She'll be in turmoil. It's a big blow to all of us. She's got the shit storm of how to manage four kids, a house, and a massive donkey-sized dog they call Pipsqueak. I'm in awe that she even managed to get out of bed this morning.

"Melinda, you know you don't have to be my dating guru? I'm grateful and all, but you know, some quality time with my favourite girl is probably all I need, yeah?"

"Oh honey, you know I love doing this stuff. Besides, I was all fired up for a wedding, but then you finally went and dumped Incompetent Chris. So, we're finding you a plan B. What the hell is that loud music?"

"Oh, that? It's just payback for my noisy neighbour. Are you sure you're okay?" I turn the music down.

"Yes, yes. I'm fine. Are you okay? Not missing Callous Chris I hope?"

"I'm fine," I automatically say, but realise it's true. "To be honest, apart from seeing crap-head on Facebook with a new chick, I'm A-okay." I grimace. How dare he meet someone else first!

"Listen, I really do have to go. Ed's trying to feed Pip Chocó pops and you know what his constitution is like. We'll have turds the size of turkeys if I'm not quick. Call me tonight, but Joanie?"

"Yeah?"

"You will be just fine. You're gorgeous, you don't realise how much so, and when I put out the word you were single, I had guys biting my arm off to take you out. You're quite the catch."

"You did what-"

"Got to go, speak to you later..."

The line goes dead.

I flip the music to angry loud rock and continue to get ready for work. When I'm showered, I put on my cute little pixie boots, some red tights, and a short-ish black skirt. My white blouse is semi translucent and hugs my breasts in just the right way and my dark hair hangs loose just past my breasts. I push my geeky specs up my nose and smile at myself in the mirror. Despite being under-slept and under-sexed, I decide I look good enough and after switching the music off, I head for the door. My note serves as a convenient reminder and I check the peephole.

All clear.

I step out and take a big sniff of the air.

Two stands opposite me, his poodle in hand. "Hi Bruce, nice morning for a walk?" I ask.

"Ah Joanie, it's blowing a Hooley out there. Bit frosty too. Be careful you don't slip and break a hip." He winks and opens his standard edition red door and escapes inside. I wave him off, despite my offense that he thinks I'm of an age that I could break a hip.

I shake the thought and am ready to stomp off when my foot tangles in a dark grey T-shirt. Six's T-shirt.

I consider my options. I could fold it neatly and leave it outside his door as a reminder of his cheeky little display last night—it plays on repeat in my mind. My brain heats to a simmer and my thoughts darken.

I could throw it in the dumpster at the side of our building, or even roll it around in Two's poodles lasting essence, or...

I pick up the shirt and balance it on the end of my index finger, careful not to inhale it, and walk the ten paces to the door beside mine. A door so closely imitated but dirtier. He hasn't cleaned it since he moved in.

I tap the steel knocker hard, six times and wait. I stare into the peephole, keeping my smugness inside and practice my best I know what you did last night pose.

Even though I'm waiting for it, I'm taken aback when the door finally opens.

Six stands in front of me, leaning against the jar of the door. He's wearing just a tight pair of cotton boxer briefs. His body is tanned. Not holiday tanned, but an even olive tone that I'm sure continues under his boxers. The gaps between his abs are only slightly lighter and emphasise the curve and dip of the hard peaks.

I want to touch them to see if they are as hard and smooth as they look, but Six coughs to remind me that he is indeed inside this mountain of man. My head blinks up to meet his.

His hair is all dishevelled. There's a pillow crease on the right side of his face. I remember the feral sounds that kept me from sleep last night and my jaw tightens.

"Four, you here for a night cap?"

"It's eight a.m." My voice is hard and I narrow my eyes to emphasise my annoyance.

I hold out his T-shirt and pin him with my most disgusted look. "You left this outside my door."

I raise my eyebrows, expecting his embarrassed look, his admission of guilt.

"Shit, Four, it's eight a.m.? I could have stopped by to grab it later."

Indignation fills me up from my feet all the way to the top of my head. Steam gushes out from my ears as I firmly tell him, "Six! Some of us work around here. Some of us need to sleep at night. Some of us do not want to hear bad corridor Karaoke, and some of us do not want to trip over—surplus to requirements—T-shirts! Don't make me bring this up at the owners' meeting. We ALL lived here in harmony before you arrived. You have to be more respectful; more responsive to the needs of all your neighbours!"

Even I'm impressed by my businesslike stance. I hike my laptop bag up onto my shoulder to emphasise my reasonable and civilised manner.

"Four, I can be as responsive to your needs as you want me to be. In fact, I think you already felt just how responsive I could be. But shit, it's eight a.m... a man needs sleep..."

Two opens his door to see what all the commotion is

about. "Can you two keep it down? I've got a date later and I want to be well-rested for it!" Two adjusts his trousers and pushes his slippery toupee back into place.

Six waggles his eyebrows and grins. "Sure, Two—just a lovers tiff, you go rest your jets." He winks and I watch Two wink back as if high fiving across the hall.

My anger heightens and I whisper a cuss. "Look, please just keep the noise and the mess to a minimum!" I shove the T-shirt in his hand and spin on my heel to walk away. He seems to have no recollection of his singing karaoke show outside of my door last night. I bet he remembers Twenty alright though.

"Hey Four..."

My face swings back too keenly.

"Nice legs!"

I narrow my eyes and curse, "Sexist Pig!"

I turn my face back to the direction I am heading and a small smile creeps on my face. Yes, my legs do look good today. I take bigger strides just to show them off.

Please, God, let tonight's date be nice.

Chapter 5

I know I'm over-dressed when I walk into the Brit and notice I'm the only person not wearing some type of polyester sports attire.

The bar is wall-to-wall television screens playing every sport known to mankind. The patrons are all dressed in football kits in every colour of the rainbow. Most of them are holding beers and pay me no attention what-so-ever as they yell and call out to whichever TV screen they're supporting.

What was Melinda thinking, setting this up as a date?

I scan the room for someone in a hat. I have three options. An elderly chap in a peek cap sits in the corner of the bar, clutching his unlit pipe in one hand and a mug of beer in the other.

It can't be him; she wouldn't do that to me, surely.

On the other side of the room is a guy closer to my own age, maybe a few years younger. He has a bright red football shirt on; he's thrashing his arms around and growling obscenities at the ref. His face is bright red too; it also matches the red cups on his two-cupped hat that's feeding beer straight into his mouth.

I'm dying.

Please, no.

"Hey Joanie." A light finger taps me on my arm. "Thought I'd better come say hello before you balked from the building."

"Matt?" I squint, checking it really is him. I haven't seen Matthew Deer since I left school. He was captain of the football team and way out of my league back then. He's carrying a baseball hat with his team's football logo on it. The relief is so acute I feel a smile light up my face. He's aged well, slightly thinner in the hair department than I remember but still, he's got to be six-foot-four and built like a Russian shot putter. He still works out, judging by the network of veins popping out of his enormous biceps.

"It's good to see you." Matt leans in for a hug, and I oblige by awkwardly holding him against me for a second. I look back at his square jaw and childlike wondering eyes.

"Shall we take a seat? Game starts at half-past and this place will fill up quick."

"Sure," I agree. This might not be so bad. At least we should have things to talk about, people in common at least.

"I'll get us both a beer," Matt offers, and I tell him just a Coke for me since I brought the car.

We're off to a good start. On my first date with Chris, I bought the drinks, the food, and paid the tip. The complete opposite of Chris, that's what I'm looking for.

Matt returns and we settle into an easy discussion about where we're at following school. He tells me all about his job at the football stadium. Sometimes he gets cheap tickets and the length of the grass absolutely cannot be longer than five centimetres on match day. I listen with rapt interest nodding and agreeing with his energetic account of what it's like to be responsible for whether the game is a success or a failure. After all, if the pitch is not mowed to absolute precision, who will they hold to account? Matt, that's who.

"So you work in a real office, wow, what's that like?" he asks.

I start to tell him, over the noise of the punters singing match games and being abusive to the ref on TV, that I work in accounts at Dean and Molver. Matt looks mildly interested before he checks his watch and holds up his hand to pause me.

"The game is just about to start. Do you want another drink?"

As nice as it is of him to offer me another drink, I can't help but think if this is his level of attention now, where will we be in ten years time when the kids have the pox and I've broken my leg walking the dog because Matt's too busy at the football.

"Actually Matt, I've got a headache coming on so I think I'll just go home. Thanks for the drink."

"Oh. You sure?"

"Yeah. It was good to see you though. Enjoy the game."

We say our goodbyes and I leave the bar feeling more dejected than ever. If Matt is a sample of the available offerings, I'd better start researching whether Siamese or Persian's live the longest.

When I reach my car, I dial Melinda. "Matt flipping Deer. Seriously? I could have picked a better suitor in the cleaning cupboard at work. Somewhere between the dish soap and wet rags! You know the date was at a bar, to watch the football. I hate football. No more, Melinda. No more dates without me vetting them first."

"What? Oh, yeah your date. You finished already?" She sounds quieter than usual. Her normally strong voice is devoid of its usual confidence. I'm about to check if she is okay when she continues. "Okay, okay, so he wasn't your type. I'm uploading the data into the algorithm. The next one will be better I promise. You've got to admit he is pretty to look at."

I soften; she is just trying to help.

"Pretty dim, yes. Look, why don't we meet for coffee? Stop this nonsense and have a proper chat. It feels like ages since we've properly caught up."

"Can't, I've got too much on. Besides, Mikey is at his weeklong intense cookery class at the community centre. It wouldn't be fair if you gave up now, and the next guy is so much better. I put Matt first because he was at least familiar. I thought it would break you in gently."

"I'm not a horse!" I tell Melinda. "Surely this is a disaster idea. Can't I just meet someone the organic way?"

"Well you could, but I was hoping that I wouldn't have to tell you this, I noticed that Chris has changed his status to engaged. Joanie, I'm sorry."

Fire boils the liquid that encases my brain and I'm ready to explode.

"He did what?"

"It's the blonde. It'll never last, babe. I was so angry I left five bad reviews on his crap app from every device in the house. I'm trying to find his address to send him a parcel of Ed's vomit from this morning. He won't get away with this!"

I try to respond but I'm dumb struck. He's known her just a few days and he already proposed. We were together three years. Am I so unlovable?

"Joanie, you there? Don't you dare internalize this. Whoever she is, she doesn't even know what a lowlife loser he is. This is not about you. You are kind, funny, and beautiful and you will find someone deserving of you. Right now, you need to find your war face. Screw him; you had a lucky escape. You hear me?"

I wonder if that is what Melinda is doing. Putting on her war face, seeing lawyers and preparing for the battle that is divorce.

"Thanks. It's been a long day. I think I am going to go home and take a bubble bath. I'm okay, really I am. I'm putting on my angry face right now."

"Good. I'll email you the details for tomorrow's date.

Love you."

She hangs up.

I select my angriest playlist and flip the car into reverse. I'm not sure whether the other road users can sense my rage, but the roads are clear and I get home in record time. When I approach my usual space, the one I can see from my kitchen window, a red haze fills my vision. Someone has parked in my usual space. A matte black muscle car with tires the width of a tractor's sits smugly in my spot.

I drive around the small area, where twenty parking spaces are neatly drawn out to find that there is not one single space available. In the spot next to mine, where the owner of apartment six would normally park, is a shiny, mean-looking Harley Davidson motorcycle.

In my heart of hearts, I know it's not a visitor's car. It's Six's car. I want to ram it with my own. I wonder if I did, would Six run out and I could mow him down too? I don't do it. I like my VW beetle and it would be a shame to dent her on the basis of one selfish resident.

When I get inside my apartment, I switch on my laptop and pull up a new group email, which I address to the generic Owners Society. We use it for building related issues like the annual BBQ, and for the attention of the person whose dog keeps urinating in the downstairs hall.

I start typing as politely as I can, though the rage projects through my fingers, and I use the search and find function to remove several words starting with F.

To whom it may concern,

The parking space adjacent to the storage bins is and has always been the earmarked spot for apartment FOUR.

Imagine my dismay to find that not only has someone taken my space today, but it seems ALL of the available spaces have been taken. As I'm sure you are all aware, the owner's handbook states that there is enough parking spaces for ONE car each. Therefore, I would politely request that the car be removed, with immediate effect, and is never again put in my space. As it is, it was raining and I had to walk two blocks from Merson Street and my suede boots are now ruined!

Yours,

Four

I feel better after my rant. I put the laptop on the sofa and venture into the kitchen and pour a glass of wine. While running a bath, the ping of an incoming message sounds from my laptop.

Two emails: One from Melinda and one from Six.

Dear Four,

Please do not get your knickers in a twist. It is just a car. I think you'll find that, while the handbook points out that there are enough spaces, it doesn't suggest you have your own. Besides, Two doesn't own a car. He said I am welcome to use his space for my motorcycle.

The spaces are not numbered, so I have no idea who took the last space.

Regards,

Six

I fume a reply:

No, Six. You are right. They are not numbered, but they are in fact, designated. Please do not do this again.

Four

When an hour goes by without a retort, I relax and am finally able to enjoy my bath and wine.

There! That showed him. No one messes with Joanie Fox anymore!

Chapter 6

As soon as I wake, I start to read Melinda's itinerary for tonight's date.

You will meet Brett at eight p.m. at the Dizzying Heights Bistro at the top of Pleasure Point. Wear your petrol blue dress with your skyscraper heels. I've ordered a taxi to pick you up at seven-forty-five so you can have a glass of wine and relax.

I scan the column marked additional information. Brett Tomlin is a thirty-two year old investment banker. He drives a blue BMW and has a cat named Barry. On weekends, Brett volunteers at his mother's cat shelter and he likes to go sailing.

I have to admit that on paper, this one looks good. Being kind to animals, helpful to his mother, and healthy pastimes are all bonuses. It has to be better than riding a motorcycle, pissing off your neighbours and parking in other people's spaces!

The date location compensates for my earlier reluctance, and I feel flips of excitement in my tummy. Dizzying Heights has been open six months now and has been impossible to get reservations at. I should know, Chris had been desperate for a meet with the owner, who he had heard was some big-shot businessman.

Dizzying Heights is located at the top of a local beauty spot, where lovers come to kiss and the depressed come to jump. It overlooks the sea, which is just a fifteen-minute walk from here.

Melinda did good.

After a pleasant day at work, I'm able to put thoughts

of Chris and his new fiancée to the back of my mind, I ate a wholesome lunch and got an express manicure in my lunch hour in preparation for tonight.

As I pull up to my apartment building, I'm feeling better than ever. Even the grey sky can't dampen my mood. I reverse into my space in one fluid manoeuvre and am impressed with my skilful parking. The foyer door glides open with only the slightest of shoves and I sniff the air. It is a cold assault of my nostrils, with only the freshness of the damp air outside. No woody scent of Six or floral assault of Twenty.

I'm feeling so chipper, I practically skip down the hall to my apartment.

After showering and putting on my petrol blue dress, as instructed by Mel, I add a few curls to my hair to add some volume and leave it loose. I set it with a spray of lacquer and put on my make-up, opting for a deep red lip and a nude eye. My lips look full and plump, and I wonder if my date will be kiss worthy.

At seven-thirty, my silver clutch bag is packed and my cashmere shrug is wrapped around my shoulders. The wind howls against my window to remind me it's Baltic outside, but I decide I don't care. As a precaution, I slip my umbrella under my arm because my massive parker coat would totally ruin the Sex Siren vibe that I'm going for. I just hope Brett Tomlin is worthy of all this effort.

After checking the peephole, I step out into the corridor and walk to the frigid foyer. My taxi should be here soon. There are heavy footsteps on the carpet behind me, and I swing my head around to check the source of my distraction. Six looms in front of me. He's wearing a bright white button down shirt, a smart black trouser, and carrying the matching suit jacket over his right arm. He stops beside me, his head cocked to one side, a slight curve to his lips.

"Four."

I nod in acknowledgement. "Six."

He nods back. I feel his eyes slide over me and his brows lift in what I think is a glint of appreciation. I nibble my lip, nervous and excited that he's checking me out. Six puts on his jacket and my eyes graze across his cotton-sheathed torso. I gulp a little as I pull the archived memory of Six's wet chest. His eyes catch mine looking, and he grins a knowing smile. I take a step forward and jut out my chin.

Six is so childish.

We both stare out of the floor to ceiling glass doors, watching the rain lash down via the glow of the streetlight.

Six holds something out in his hand for me to view. It's a piece of white lined paper that has a pretty, pink print-lace edge across all four corners. Scrawled on the sheet of the notepaper are the words: Check for ~~sex~~ Six!!!

Recognition sparks a furnace inside my cheeks.

"I believe this must be yours?"

Trust Six to be a smug bastard.

I bet he has something similar on his door.

"Never seen it before in my life," I say, snatching it off him and tucking it in my clutch.

Please taxi, I beg, don't be your usual tardy self.

"Hot date tonight then, Four?" The heat of Six's stare warms my cheeks, but I refuse to look back at him.

"Wouldn't you like to know, Six." I deadpan, continuing to stare at the rain.

"I hope it's inside. We're set for a storm."

"That's none of your business, Six."

"Well, I think a storm is everybody's business, Four. I see the lady isn't as sweet as her perfume tonight." There's a dark humourous vibe to Six's words.

My umbrella is difficult to grip in my sweating palms, and the foyer feels like a pressure cooker. If I turn to make eye contact, my make-up might melt and slide right off my face.

"You're rather nervous. A first date, perhaps? Or maybe…" I hear Six's hand scruff against his chin. "Four, are you going on a blind date?"

A growl sneaks past my teeth as my head shakes of its own volition. How am I so easy to read?

"No, no I'm not going on a blind date. Not that it is any of your concern. Perhaps you should pay more mind to your own affairs. Where is the delightful Twenty anyway?"

"Twenty? I'm not sure I know where Twenty is. You're not, wait, are you jealous, Four?"

My face lurches at his audacity. "Jealous? Me?" I cough out an almighty laugh. "Why on earth would I be jealous? I hardly know you, and what I do know is that I don't like you. I don't like you parking your car in my space, or you lowering the tone with your drunken displays, and I don't like being woken up in the middle of the night by the laughing hyena!"

Six's eyebrows rise with the corners of his mouth and he nods. "You are quite the peeping Tom, aren't you? It's okay. I completely understand. Rest assured, I will keep the noise down in future. Let you get a good night's rest."

Six's index finger moves cautiously to the underside of my chin as he gently nudges my mouth shut. I jump backwards and am suddenly blinded by the headlights of the oncoming taxi as it swings around the water feature out front, coming to a stop in front of the foyer doors.

"Goodbye, Six."

"See you soon, Four. Enjoy your date."

I push the door open and my hair is blasted skyward by the wind.

"None of your business, Six."

What he calls back is impossible to hear clearly because of the sheer velocity of the wind, but it sounded a lot like, "Could be if you wanted it to be, Four."

***

I arrive at Dizzying Heights ten minutes late after the

taxi driver, a stout man in his fifties, who smelled of coffee and hand rolled cigarettes, took the cautious route away from the coastline. The sky crackled and boomed the whole way. My driver looked nervous as hell to be out in this weather and took the long, tree lined, winding road up to Dizzying Heights at a pace only a few miles above walking speed. When we reached the top, I was awestruck and took longer to take my cash from my purse to admire the skyline. From up here you could see for miles. Our whole town, just a sprinkling of glittering lights down below, and beyond that the sea where a hell-fire storm was thundering above us. When the driver coughed nervously, I paid him and made my way up the stairs into the old stately home that was now an exclusive restaurant and bar.

Inside, it is decadently styled. The porcelain floors are so mirror-like my thighs clench to prevent flashing the front of house. A huge chandelier hangs from the grand ceiling, which is framed by a double sweeping staircase.

There's a tall mahogany carved desk to my left that sits on a raised platform. Three staff members look down on arriving guests and take turns greeting and escorting them to their destinations. I smile at the handsome young gentleman who has met my eye; his name badge is almost in view when someone gently cups my elbow.

I turn with a smile to greet my escort.

"Six?"

"Ah, Four. What might you be doing here?"

I look back to the young gentleman whose name badge I cannot see. Six ushers him away, leaving me at his mercy. I signal to him to come back, that I do in fact require his assistance. He skirts just out of arms reach, waiting for Six's approval.

"It's okay, this is my good friend, Four. I can do the honours, Jim." He gives the man a curt nod, silently sending him on his way. "Do you have a reservation?"

"Six, are you stalking me? Should I file a restraining order?"

"No, Four. This is my place. I could have driven you here had you mentioned you were coming. Reservation?"

"Oh." Electric shocks creep up my spine and heat my neck as Six takes my shrug from around my shoulders. He puts two fingers on the small of my back to guide me through the entrance hall. "So, you work here?" I check.

"No Four, this is my place. I own it. I am the boss. You are officially worshiping at my alter, how does it feel?" he asks.

I gulp and follow his lead.

"It makes sense, great big ostentatious building, for great big-headed bastard. Did they raise the ceilings especially?"

I grin, pleased with myself. I managed some kind of retort, given how impressed I am with his business.

Six holds my arm to pause me when we arrive at another desk by the doors to the restaurant. "Now then, Four, what name is the reservation? Will I finally learn your name?"

I smile smugly. No he will not.

"The reservation is in the name of Brett Tomlin."

Six skims the sheet of paper in front of him, his face unreadable. "Ah, Mr. Tomlin. Oh." Six scratches the scruff on his chin. "Could you describe him, please? You see we have two guests with that name."

I try to breathe steadily despite having no clue of the answer. The heat of panic creeps up my spine. In just a moment, he's going to know for sure that I'm on a blind date if I don't find something convincing to say.

"It's okay, Four. Just kidding, only one Mr. Tomlin's here tonight."

Steam blows from my ears, and I flick Six's hand away and walk ahead when he tries to guide me through the doors. If I was nervous before, I'm terrified now. What if my date is some heinous looking monster with a square head and round body? What if he is sixty years old and has hairy hands?

I turn to look back at the exit and wonder if I can make an escape.

"Don't be nervous, Four. You look beautiful."

I stumble but am able to right myself before Six catches my arm. What did he say that for? Is he trying to put me on edge, make my heart jump out of my chest?

Six leads me through the restaurant towards huge windows that overlook the dimly lit lawn that I know leads down to the cliff edge and sea beyond.

Above the volume of the piano music, the clouds growl as they continue their angry torment of the sea. The contrast is strangely ambient as the other diners sit at candlelit tables, closely hugged to their partners.

"Hello, you." Brett Tomlin stands with a toothy grin and holds out a hand. It's a polite if not slightly awkward gesture, perfect for a first meeting, but sadly confirming Six's suspicions that we don't know each other from Adam.

I smile and nod a hello as Brett's smooth hand takes mine and gives it a friendly squeeze. He has darkly tanned skin, bright white teeth and black hair that curls at the edges.

In my peripheral vision, Six's jaw hardens as he assesses Brett.

"I'll leave you both to it." Six clears his throat and walks away.

I sit opposite a sharp and suave looking Brett. He's wearing a well-cut navy shirt that is turned up at the sleeves. The sheen of the material is pulled tight, alluding to the promise of heavy-set biceps.

I begin the evening feeling nervous that Six can see us but soon feel more relaxed as I get talking to Brett. He pours me a large glass of red wine from the bottle he has already ordered, and I start the evening by asking if he had a good day.

Brett is confident and well mannered. He apologises for the weather and we both admire our front row seats for the storm. Lightening crackles and pops as it looms closer.

The menu is worded entirely in French and sensing my concern, Brett asks, "Shall we just order two steaks and some fries?" He puts his menu down at the side of his cutlery and leans forward on his hands, taking me in.

I mirror him. "Actually, I think that's exactly what I fancy tonight."

"You look pretty," he says. His eyes look almost black in the candlelight. I flush as I feel them skim across my body, and I nibble my lip, not used to this kind of attention. My nerve endings are ablaze as Brett touches my hand, refilling my glass.

Brett's attention is directly on me when he asks about my job, my family and my friends. Even in the early days with Chris, I never fully had his undivided attention, there was always something distracting him. And so, with Brett's encouragement, I talk.

I gush about my job, my family, and my friends, which leaves me to explain, "So you see, Melinda set up these ten dates. I don't know if I'll go on all of them, ten is a little crazy after all, but she's put in so much effort. I don't know I... Maybe I feel like I need to validate her effort." I stutter an embarrassed giggle, hoping he doesn't think I'm a massive harlot. "I'm not having sex with any of them, though. I'd never put out on the first date, in case you were expecting... or wondering." My skin catches on fire, and I'm tempted to face plant my head in my hands.

God I sound ridiculous.

"Joanie, I would never expect a woman to put out on the first date," Brett replies. His eyes lit with fascination. "You should go on the dates. Three years is a long time in a relationship. Maybe she thinks you need to play the field, weigh up your options, and not settle for the first guy that comes around. Which date number am I, out of interest?"

I'm surprised at how well he takes the details of my task.

"You are number two. But, I have to say you are the best, so far." I giggle.

The grin on Brett's already smiling face widens. "I do love a challenge." He winks. "I already know I'd really like to see you again. Can I have your phone number?"

I consider for a moment and then take my phone from my bag. Brett takes his out too and we exchange numbers.

A glass shatters above the noise of the thunder, and I catch Six in the corner of my eye reprimanding a member of the waiting staff.

When our meal is finished, Brett insists on paying the bill and then escorts me to the grand entrance. Out of the bubble that our table in the restaurant provided, I feel vulnerable and exposed. My eyes search of their own accord for Six. Other diners are leaving, either braving the heavy winds and icy sleet to go outside to their cars or awaiting taxi's, and others use the opulent, curved staircases to head upstairs. I nosily peer after them wondering where they are going.

I look at my new watch and sigh.

I'm disappointed to notice it's only ten p.m.

"Thank you for a lovely evening." Brett's eye contact is intense and my stomach does a flip. It has been a lovely evening, and I decide to text Melinda to commend her good effort.

Brett, having retrieved my shrug, wraps it around my shoulders. He's quite a few inches taller than I am, and I have to angle my face up towards his to maintain eye contact.

I'm about to respond, to agree that it was a lovely evening, when I'm almost bowled over by Six. As he nudges me, Six steadies me by holding my right arm. Brett isn't as fortunate and he is forced to take a step back, or be bumped on his backside by Six.

"Good, you're still here. Sorry Brad, I'm going to have to steal your date. Four, I'll give you a lift home tonight. I forgot my keys."

Brett steps forward and loops my left arm. "Actually, I was going to offer to drive her home."

"Hmm." Six strokes the scruff of his jaw as he eyes up Brett and then nods. "That could work. Give me a minute, I'll get my jacket."

"Actually, we're on a date, that wouldn't be convenient," Brett corrects Six and my mouth pops open. Brett's got balls! My eyes widen at Six as I wait for his retort.

"Of course, you're right. I'm sorry, what was I thinking? So, Brody, was that two whole bottles of wine Four here drank to herself?"

Six then turns to me as if to chastise. "Four, what have I told you about binge drinking?"

My mouth hangs open, unable to formulate a retort, while Six continues his chatter, "It's like when I found Four's shoe in the hallway last week. I told her getting so wasted that you lose a shoe does not make you Cinderella, more like gives you liver failure." Six tuts, and his hand holds his hip.

I glare to my left at Six. "I didn't drink all the wine tonight." I swing an apologetic glance to Brett and shake my head to reinforce my comments. "And I don't binge drink."

Mostly, I silently add.

"Oh, you didn't drink all the wine this time? Good for you, Four. So how much did you drink, Barry?"

I'm about to flip my lid and tell Six to get lost, when Brett says, "Only a couple of glasses. I'm fine to drive, and my name is Brett."

"Oh. Just a couple, huh?" Six nods his head.

I count back. Brett had more than I did. I stopped him topping up my glass a few times and he ended up finishing the second bottle.

"Maybe you shouldn't drive," I tell Brett.

Brett nod's in reply. Now that I look at him, he does seem a bit red faced and a little less steady on his feet.

Six may have just saved me from getting in a car with a drunk driver.

"Go see Suzy at reception; she'll organise you a taxi." Six tells Brett with a wink and pulls me by my arm. "Come along Four, let's try getting you home with both shoes intact this time."

I mouth the word sorry to Brett as I'm pulled along by Six. I'm unsure how Six has managed to untangle me from Brett, who stands mouth agape watching Six usher his date out of the heavy doors. Equally, I don't know if I should be furious or thankful for his intervention. My mind is in shock, but the drive home is the perfect place to demand answers.

Chapter 7

Six opens the door of his car and waits expectantly for me to clamber inside. The car is sporty and black; its seats are just a few inches above ground level. I assess the likelihood of getting in without exposing my backside to the world and to Six.

"Come on Four, my balls are freezing off out here."

"I didn't ask for your intervention. I could have gotten a taxi."

"Ah, but who could resist a gentleman such as me." Six's expression is jovial and his mouth turns up at the side, revealing just a hint of a dimple.

I narrow my eyes at Six as I get in the car. I get in, not because of Six's prompting, but because the bitter wind is whooshing my dress up and the silk of my knickers is starting to freeze against my ass.

The door slams shut and Six jogs around to the driver's side. The wind blasts his hair in all directions but instead of looking a mess, he has the look of a model in a commercial. I cross my arms in a huff.

Trust Six to make storms look sexy.

Six drops down into the seat beside me and pushes the

key into the ignition. The car roars to life so loudly that the other users of the car park stop—even though the rain is turning to hail—and look at the car. I comb my hair across my face to obscure their view.

Trust Six to have an attention-whore of a car.

"You like my car, huh Four?" Six nibbles the corner of his plump lower lip as he waits for my answer.

Sitting so close to the chassis is a new experience for me. The vibrations from the engine seep through my seat and into my bones. It's strangely relaxing and a little erotic.

"It's ostentatious and smells of old leather, and you," I respond.

Six pushes on the accelerator and my stomach is left behind in the thrill. I grip the sides of the leather sports seat as Six manoeuvres the car down the winding private driveway down to the coastal road below. My ears pop and an electrical current runs up my body as Six navigates the car onto the empty road and picks up speed.

"That's better, Four. It's good to see you smile. You're always so uptight. You should relax more."

I throw him an angry glare.

"I am not uptight. I was relaxed, Six, on my date. The one you sabotaged, by the way."

"I'm not apologising for that. You shouldn't be getting into cars with men you don't know, or drunk drivers, for that matter. You're smarter than that."

A growl escapes my lips. He is infuriating.

"I hadn't even agreed that Brett could take me home. You barged in and interfered, and the next thing I know I'm stuck in a car with Sanctimonious Six!"

"Why do you always say 'Six' like it's a dirty word? Would you like to know my real name?"

The number is not dirty, but the places he takes my thoughts to are one hundred percent filthy. I desperately want to know his name, but I would never ask. The fear of what it may do to my level of constraint around him is a risk I'm unwilling to take.

"No, Six, I do not want to know your name."

"Fair enough, though frankly, Four, I've wondered quite a lot about your name. The beautiful woman with the cute glasses and freckles; I wonder if she is a Mabel or a Sue?" he teases. "Perhaps she is a Jane or a… no definitely not, too fiery to be a plain Jane."

Too soon, we turn the corner into our building's driveway. Of course, there is a space right next to the front entrance for Six to slide into; Six is accustomed to strokes of luck.

"Why do you tease me so much, Six?" I ask.

"You grind my gears, too. I guess your responses are fascinating to me, Four."

I nod and stare at our building. I can't work out if fascinating is good. Some people might use the word fascinating in reference to mould, fungus, or genital warts.

Six opens my car door and helps me out by holding my hand. This low to the ground, a little help is essential or else I may be stuck here forever; his hand is smooth, his fingers long and firm.

I follow him to the entrance where he keys the lock and pushes the door open. Trust Six to open the door with ease.

As we meander towards our respective doors, we both stop beside mine and Six fishes his apartment key from his pocket in preparation. A smile caused by the knowledge that I caught him out graces my features and I say, "I see you found your keys, huh, Six?"

"Would you look at that," Six grins knowingly. "They were in my pocket the whole time."

I look up and study Six's face. He didn't need to intervene tonight, but I'm glad he did. It didn't occur to me that Brett might be too drunk to drive.

Really, I suppose, it was quite sweet.

"Thanks, for the lift, Six," I say and my hands rest up on Six's shoulder as I tiptoe to plant a kiss on the side of his scruffy jaw, but Six's face moves and I catch the soft, full part of his lips square-on. My weary lips are, for a second, torn against resting on the soft pillow his lips provide, or jumping inside of my mouth to take cover.

Six's eyes widen like saucers, and I leap out of his reach in shock that I, Four, just kissed Six, the sexy bastard!

Six's hands bunch in his pockets and he nods, acknowledging. A smile plays on his lips and I wait for his teasing.

My words spew in a splutter, trying to salvage what remains of my dignity. "I didn't mean to… You moved. That was your fault. I um… I just wanted to say thanks for the ride, that's all."

As I turn my key in the lock of my door, Six finds his voice. "You know if you wanted to kiss me you just had to ask, Four. My lips are at your disposal."

"In your dreams, Six." I walk into my apartment and close the door behind me.

In the back draft of the door I just catch him say, "Frequently, Four. Frequently."

***

After work the next day, I'm staring into my empty fridge when the buzzer from the foyer door makes me jump.

"Hello, who is it?" I sing.

"Super Hot Guy."

"Super Hot Guy, who?" I ask, teasingly.

"Super Hot Guy, who has 'thrice baked' lasagne, from scratch I might add, pasta and all. Let me in, Joanie, before the dish lasers off my fingerprints!"

"Come-on in then Mikey, though I think Super Hot Guy is a stretch."

I giggle and buzz him in. I put my internal door on the latch and, while I wait for him to reach my apartment, I change out of my work clothes, opting for some yoga pants and a vest top for comfort, and switch the kettle on to boil.

"Incredibly hot, available guy brings incredibly hot, fricking lasagne," Mikey squeals as he dances through the hallway and into my apartment. He drops the container on the dining table and falls back on the adjacent sofa.

"That was exhausting," he says. "Why people don't just eat at restaurants instead of putting themselves through all that I'll never know."

"So you're enjoying intense cookery one-oh-one then?" I chuckle; he's red in the face and panting. Mikey hasn't sweat this much since the rumour broke that One Direction were splitting up.

"Joanie, it was awful," Mikey whines. "Chef made us make ten different types of pasta. He's all anal, and not in a good way, about the hand rolling of the dough and making it the right thickness. Is it a crime to prefer a long, thick noodle, Joanie, is it? Because I didn't think so, but Chef, Chef likes them long and thin. He thinks I add too much salt. Me? I pride myself on just the right ratio of sodium to liquid, but Chef said he's worried about my arteries. I told him, 'my arteries are in the best shape of their life.'"

"And relax." I pass Mikey a cup of the herbal tea that I keep just for him. "So you don't like the cookery class then?" I ask.

"It's okay. It's been quite a distraction, you know, with Ted going back to his wife."

My mouth gawks open.

"He went back to his wife? You poor thing, why didn't you say?"

"You were so upset about Chris and I didn't want to steal your misery. Besides, he'll be on his hands and knees, begging me back before long, same as always."

This is true. Ted has been married for twenty years; he's been with Mikey for eleven of those, and someone else before that.

"Thank you for allowing me to wallow in my misery,

but you can tell me anything. Even if I'm heartbroken, I want to know. I'm still annoyed with Melinda for keeping her split with Steve a secret."

Mikey grabs plates from the kitchen and starts to dish up the lasagne and a salad from the Tupperware container he has brought. As he loads it on the plate, my mouth salivates and my hunger growls.

"Actually, I have news. Steve is back. It's part of the reason I'm here. Melinda decided to come to cookery with me, and when we got back to Melinda's place, Steve's car was in the driveway, so I let her out and said I'd come here instead, to give them chance to reconnect after his 'business trip.'"

Mikey only plates me a small amount, reminding me I have a date tonight. Over dinner, we debate whether Steve and Melinda will get back together, and why they might have broken up in the first place.

I invite Mikey to stay in my spare bedroom until Steve goes away again, or until Mikey is ready to go home. He hates being alone in his apartment, so his stay may wind up being a while.

I'm just about to fill Mikey in on tonight's date, when a deep, brassy noise interrupts our conversation.

"What is that God-awful noise?" Mikey asks.

"That, my friend, is Six, playing his trombone. It's a recent thing, designed to destroy me, but I am not letting it. No. It started last night, went on until late, and then started up again this morning. However, I have a cunning plan."

I get up, and move the speakers of my docking station, resting them on top of the headboard in my bedroom. Mikey stands back, and his shoulders bob as he chuckles.

"I think some Dolly Parton may be in order," I announce, proud of my retaliation.

Letting Dolly sing her heart out to the audience of my blank wall, I collect a fresh set of clothes and shut the door, leaving Dolly alone in the bedroom.

"That's better. I'll be in the bathroom getting ready for my date. You can stay as long as you like, Mikey, but you do not take Dolly off repeat. You hear me?"

"Amen to that sister," Mikey says and sings along to Dolly.

***

I slam the door as I walk back in my apartment praying to God there is more lasagne left and wine. I definitely need wine after a terrible date number three.

"That was the worst. No more. I'm telling Melinda, NO MORE," I yell to Mikey as I walk into the lounge.

"Four, you look all discombobulated. Let me put some music on to help you relax. My personal favourite, Jolene? Or would you prefer Nine to Five?"

Six, the smug bastard, looks relaxed sitting on my sofa, smiling his face off with his bare feet resting on my coffee table. Mikey stands in the doorway of the adjacent kitchen with a cup in his hand.

"What's going on?" My eyes tighten on Mikey, who stands immobilised like a rabbit about to become a stew.

"I didn't mean to let him in, Joanie. He came about the music, but then he smelled the lasagne."

I let out a slow, controlled breath.

It's okay.

I can be calm.

There's no need to kill anyone tonight.

Mikey shrugs out his palms, as though the situation got out of his control.

I waver. Six is a despicable character; Mikey is flaky and easily led.

Trust Six to manipulate him into letting him in.

I'm not going to let it spoil my supper. Walking into the kitchen, I open the cupboard and pour a large glass of red.

"Not for me thanks, I'm-" I fix Mikey with a death

stare.

"Mikey, please get me my lasagne."

Mikey's face is blank; he's lost for words.

A shadow looms over me. Six has moved off the sofa and is standing in the doorway of the kitchen, leaning against the door jam. In his hands is an empty glass dish. It has a smear of tomato sauce and a smattering of the cheese crust welded to the edge.

I take a long slug of my wine.

I remind myself to stay calm.

Calm, logical people don't get worked up over lasagne.

"How was the date?" Mikey chimes, removing the dish from Six and hiding it away in the dishwasher.

"Ah yes, how was your date? Date number three, wasn't it? Your home very early, Four, are you okay?"

I can't possibly tell Six that my date met me outside of the multiplex cinema, only to explain that he had arranged to get back together with his wife. He then tried to give me his telephone number, just in case their reconciliation didn't go as planned or in case I might like something 'casual.'

"I'm fine, Six. It's time you went home. I'm worn out since some jack-ass parked his car in my space again, and I had to park four streets away!" Saying it aloud reignites my anger and I slip off my heels and try very hard not to throw them at Six to hammer home the point.

"You don't own the car park, Four, but I will speak to Two's girlfriend, who has parked a mobility scooter in one of the spaces." He winks. It's a friendly, 'I got your back' wink. It makes me want to punch him in the face.

"Time you were going, Six."

Mikey throws Six a 'sorry' look and they agree that they'll see each other soon. Apparently Six has been having flying lessons, and Mikey has agreed to take him out for a lark on the local flying field.

"Okay, okay I'm leaving." Six responds to my glares by holding out his palms and then reaches to grab something from beside the sofa. I don't stare at his rock-hard, olive skin as his shirt rides up over his abs. "Thanks for the dinner, Mikey. I'll see you on the runway on Saturday. Oh, before I go, the postman left this for you earlier since you were out."

In Six's outstretched hands, barely concealed by the wet, torn, brown paper packaging is the Come-Hard-6000 in all its glory.

Trust Six to take Dolly and hit me back with the Come-Hard-6000!

"GET OUT!"

My scream is deafening.

My   blushes   are   catastrophic.

Chapter 8

After work on Friday, I end up parked almost a mile from my house. Six was right; someone is parking a mobility scooter in a perfectly good, car-sized space. Six's car is in my usual space. It makes me want to scratch the beautiful matte black paintwork, but I don't. I'm a grown-up after all. Six on the other hand is a childish asshole, and he probably can't even help it.

By the time I get into my apartment, I'm ready to throw away my Mary Jane's and amputate my own feet with a butter knife. Why do beautiful shoes have to be such deceitful divas?

I search my archives for the building contract. I go through it with beady eyes looking for evidence of Six's crimes and am furious to find residents can park in whichever space they wish. In addition, noisy sexipades are not noted as antisocial behaviours!

My phone chimes a message from Mikey. He's on his way over to my place and he wants to know if I need any groceries. Since my cupboards are empty, and my feet hurt too much to walk back to my car, I ask him to come over and pick me up to go with him to the supermarket.

At the supermarket, Mikey spends ages smelling tomatoes for freshness and fondling meat for tenderness, while I take my time checking the depth of the bottom on the wine bottles and reading the fancy descriptions on the back. I settle on some classic Chardonnay and Pinot, since I'm not brave enough to try anything new. Mikey is practicing his pizza recipe tonight. He plans to make it for a date with Chef. As such, it must be perfect.

Tonight I have dinner with date number four, and tomorrow I am going paint balling with date number five. While Sunday is usually a day of rest, I will be going to church with date number six.

"Damn it, I forgot the basil," Mikey says, once we're nearly home.

"I think I have some dried herbs in the cupboard you can use."

Mikey's face crumples in harsh creases. "I am not using dried herbs! I'll have to turn around and go back."

I laugh; he really is starting to take this cookery malarkey very seriously.

"Mikey, we're nearly home; can't you just use the dried stuff? I promise I won't tell anyone."

Mikey insists he would know. It would be cheating. "Chef says a lazy chef is a shit chef. I'll drop you here, swing back and get the herbs and meet you back at your place."

My feet rage in anger, but I reluctantly agree as Mikey swings around and stops outside my building. As I walk up the driveway toward the entrance, I notice something strange. Six's car is missing. My usual space next to the foyer is gloriously empty. My legs quicken their pace with excitement and my feet, no longer aching, break into a gallop. I have no idea what to do. My car is too far away; if I walk to retrieve it, Six might come back and take my space. I might never get it back.

So, even though the sky is a bleak shade of charcoal and there's a frigid chill in the air, I go to my space and sit on the floor in the middle of the rectangular painted white lines. I text Mikey and beg him to be quick, that I'm saving him a space. We can swap our cars over later, but I must reclaim my space.

Hours pass, perhaps days. I hug myself to keep warm and oscillate from sitting to standing. I read an article once about cold surfaces causing the onset of piles. I start to worry.

Shortly after the streetlights blink on, I hear the obnoxious thrum of Six's car turn the corner and coast towards the space I am standing in. Six sees me and flashes the lights of his car. Even though the lights blind me, I sit cross-legged on the floor. I will not be moved.

Six stops his car just a few feet away from me and gets out. I lay back, in a starfish shape, so it's more difficult for him to drag me away. He walks over and crouches beside me. I look away, refusing his eye contact and pray Mikey is close by.

"Four, you know this is a space for cars and not people?" He sounds all reasonable and chipper. He moves and puts his face in front of mine, so I cannot avoid his gaze.

Trust Six not to realise I am being defiant. I close my eyes so he cannot make me look at him.

"Four, I need to put my car in this space. I am going to need you to move."

I cross my arms and jut my chin.

Please Mikey, get here now with your sodding herbs!

"Okay, that does it."

Six's arms are giant hooks as they swing beneath my arms, and hoist… no, catapult me up and over his shoulder.

Six walks with purpose into the building. His legs move in long strides causing his glutes, clad in soft, tight denim, to lengthen and retract. Squeezing his ass right now would be a catastrophic error, so I fist and slap it instead and squeal that he should put me down.

As we pass, I call out to number eight, who is collecting her post, to please call the police because I am being attacked. She pays me no mind. She isn't wearing her usual plastic beige hearing devices around her ears today.

"Where is your key, Four?" Six asks as we approach my apartment door.

I'm not telling him they're in the pocket of my jacket. I need to break free and protect my land; I need to get back to the coveted space outside.

"Okay, have it your way," Six tells me, as if there is any chance I could have it his way.

We stride past my door all the way to his. He fumbles in his pocket and has to re-grip me, so I don't slide down his body and face plant the floor. His hand grips me by my ass; my ass doesn't seem to mind and it concentrates on staying perky under the duress. He puts his key in the lock and swings open the door with his foot.

This is it, Six is going to kill me and dispose of my body. Perhaps he'll cut me into pieces and store me in his fridge, next to the protein shakes and bloody steaks.

He walks through the hall, which is a fashionable shade of grey. He has a nice striped rug with an accent of mustard. I wonder if the police will admire it as much when they find my cold corpse rolled up inside it.

Trust Six to be current in his interior design.

My own hallway needs an update in comparison, and I realise this probably isn't the best time to have hallway envy.

My legs continue to kick and assault him as best I can. Six swings the arm that's not gripping my ass and loops his hand around my ankles. Restrained, I dangle over his shoulder like an unlucky and overgrown horseshoe.

Aware that I am losing, I change tact. "Please, don't hurt me," I beg.

Six chuckles and apologises as my head bashes the doorframe and he turns the corner into his bedroom. In one rapid lift and slide, I am thrown down onto the plush silken comforter on his bed. I land on my back, my legs akimbo.

Six looms over me, with an intense look in his eyes and a sheen of sweat coating his brow.

I swallow hard.

Trust Six to ace murderous with a side of sexy.

He takes my hands high above my head and leans forward on the bed, framing my body, his face inches from mine. "What to do with you now, naughty, defiant little Four."

Six's intense, calculating eyes match the all consuming, throbbing of his body above me. He looks like he's going to eat me.

I swallow hard, about to protest. I dislike the use of the word 'little' and I'm not sure I want to die by consumption, but something strange happens and it shuts me up.

He kisses me.

As though teaching me a lesson, Six's lips press against my own in an intense and urgent assault that's too violent to be described as a caress. The press of his mouth plants me to the bed—his bed. Magically, my mouth widens as his lips part mine, opening and closing like puppets on a string. A string that Six controls.

I'm so grateful not to be murdered, I forget the why and how and focus on the kiss, which isn't awful. It's delicious.

Trust Six to be good at kissing.

My body melds to his bed, and all I feel is the relentless pressure of his mouth against mine. Parts of my body, that I had long forgotten existed, ignite and burst into flames. If I could move, I would wave a white flag and surrender myself, it's so good.

Too good.

A traitorous groan escapes from my mouth as his sinful weight pushes down on me. I writhe beneath him to release the throb taking over my body. He feels so good and I fit right into his curves. The hand that doesn't hold my own starts a slow exploration. Six squeezes the curve of my hip and rough fingers glide up the bare skin of my torso, under my coat.

I'm suddenly too restricted in all the clothes that seemed like a good idea when I left the house earlier. I want them off, and I struggle to try to kick the toe of my boot with the other in a bid for freedom. It's the only part of my body that I have any control over and is no easy task when my legs feel so drunk and unsteady.

Six suddenly releases my mouth and the air is heaved from his lungs in a brutal choke. He releases me and falls onto his side next to me, his usual tanned face pale and drawn.

Maybe Six's stamina isn't what I had imagined. If this is his come-face, it isn't as beautiful as his cocky, sarcastic, or charming face. He looks angered and pained. Six's knees lift and he slowly rocks. Panic grips me and I jump to standing as I realise my misjudgement of the situation.

"Six, are you okay? Is it your heart?" Please God, don't let him be having a stroke. "Should I call for an ambulance?" I splutter.

Six continues to rock. His face is a ghostly white. "Shit… Four…. Knee… Balls…" Six grumbles in between shallow gasps for air.

I leap to Six's side, cupping him in my embrace, apologising empathically over, and over again. I can't believe I knee-d Six in the balls and not even on purpose!

It takes a little while for Six to compose himself, as one might expect. Once the air returns to his lungs and the colour is back in his face, Six holds his hand over mine.

"It's okay, Four. You can let go of my balls now. I think I'm going to be okay," he says, his cheeky tone returning.

I throw down the balls and leap to stand.

"I… I…" I feel the heat of blood flooding my face. I can't meet Six's gaze. It's then I notice what a nice, neatly kept bedroom he has. This room is a lighter grey than the hallway, accented in navy. It has the look of an expensive hotel. I'm suddenly eager to check out his guestroom, lounge, and kitchen—I bet his bathroom doesn't even have a leaky shower like mine.

Six stands, tall and mischievous, nibbling at his pink swollen lips; lips that just a few minutes ago had held mine like a prisoner.

"I should go," I say self-consciously, looking at the toe of my shoe, cursing its difficulty at removal.

"Yeah, I probably should too; I think I left the car running…"

Our heads lurch and snap at each other.

Our fight, the reason we are here, I have to save the space. I twist on my toes, ready to run. But Six is faster, stronger as he picks me up and throws me on the bed. By the time I am in a vertical position, Six has closed the bedroom door behind him. I hear the telltale sign of Italian leather shoes on the hardwood floor as Six runs out of his hallway slamming the door and calling out that I'll never catch him.

Trust Six to be right. I'll never catch him now.

Miffed that I won't win the car parking space battle, I take the opportunity for a very quick snoop around his bedroom.

Six folds his Calvin Kleins and neatly pairs his socks. He orders them in rows according to colour. There's not even a hint of a lonely odd sock or un-darned toe. There are no photographs or even stashes of pornography.

It's more minimalistic than animalistic.

I dig further, knowing this is not the case. In a silver box, deep in the drawer of his bedside table, Six keeps a stash of condoms. Not just any condoms, no, Six buys, as advertised on the packaging—Trend Magazine's overall winner, for four years running, in the pleasure for her and resilience categories: Stallions sheaths in an extra large, of course.

Trust Six to need giant condoms to wrap up his enormous appendage.

I continue to snoop, just for a moment, and I have a good idea.

As I smugly close the door to Six's apartment and let myself into my own, a comforting thought calms me. He may have won the battle, but the war is mine.

Chapter 9

"Four, I want my condoms and my trombone back, now!" Six calls through the door of my apartment.

"Move the car and they're yours," I taunt him, calling back through the door. Mikey gives me a questioning glance.

I ignore him.

This is his fault for needing fresh herbs. Fortunately, for Mikey, he promised to bake me homemade cookies in order to apologise.

"Not your space, Four!" Six calls back.

I mimic his voice in a childlike, squeaky voice.

"I can hear you, you know. Quit being childish and give me the condoms and the trombone or face retaliation," he threatens, as if his tantrum will spark a fear of retribution.

Instead, I play a little tune on the trombone, practising some badly blasted notes. I think I remember reading somewhere that playing the brass family of instruments improves oral sex ability. It's something to do with breathing and vibrations. I flush a little and put the trombone down.

"If you damage it, you're buying me a new one, Four.

I'm counting to six, if you don't hand back my stuff, consider it a declaration of war! One... Two... Three... Four... Five..."

Trust Six to be so self-obsessed he counts to six.

"Right, that's it. Don't say I didn't warn you," he advises. Then I hear him explain to Two that yes, he did say trombone and he's sorry to disturb him. I hear Two chuckle and the squeak of his door closing. "Four, you have been warned," Six whispers through my door.

Bring it on, Six.

***

I wake up on Saturday with a spring in my step. Last night's date, number four, wasn't what I expected, not that I was optimistic.

Peter Palmer is a professional pharmacist and founder of Voldy's Video Game Club. Peter likes Sci-Fi and Potter and arranges his hair in a bouffant, Falcon Twist on the top of his head. Sadly, for him it's thinning around the top and looks more frightened ferret than falcon funk. Having said that, he was nice, sweet even; the polar opposite to Six. He met Melinda's brother, Graham, back in 2006 at University and they have been friends ever since. He explained that he was most surprised when he received an SOS email from Melinda asking for a data analysis of all his single friends and he bravely put himself forward.

I met Peter in town. He bought us cappuccinos and we walked to the Friday Night Video Game Championships held at a local skittle hall.

Peter had been knocked out of the league following a tense tournament last week. He gave me the tour and at the end of the night, Peter said thank you for my company, but regretfully informed me that he didn't think he could ever truly feel at home with a woman who didn't know her Starship Enterprise from her Millennium Falcon. We agreed to be just friends.

***

Mikey and I spend the day preparing my hallway for a fresh coat of paint. After seeing Six's apartment, I have decided that mine badly needs updating. We sand the woodwork and cover the floor in plastic sheathing and while I head out to buy paint, Mikey bakes cookies. He's been invited over to Chef's place tonight, to experience a culinary master class and wants to take a gift to impress. Mikey doesn't mention whether there are any other guests attending, but I suspect not. Things really do seem to be hotting up in the kitchen for Mikey and Chef, and I suspect the bitching and arguing are just an act of foreplay. Unlike Six and I, who I haven't even seen since he asked for his stupid extra large condoms back.

I get to the store and back in record time, considering it's a Saturday and the shop was full of love-sick couples. Couples I don't even normally notice. I buy two tubs of prison issue grey and some white paint for the ceiling.

Normally, I'd be impatient to get started, but tonight I have date number five and I don't want to turn up with paint in my hair.

"Oh my, they smell amazing," I remark as I come through the door. "I could smell them from the foyer, top marks, Mikey. You are really getting the hang of the baking. I'm so proud of you. Now, let me at these cookies."

"Do you mind if I get in the shower first? I don't want to be late for Chef, he goes all Gordon Ramsey on the tardy kids. There's a plate of cookies for you on the counter," he sings.

I'm starving and since tonight's date is a meal, I only had a light lunch. I check my newly purchased, highly coveted watch. I'm being picked up at seven. It's almost six already but since Mikey is practically fizzing with excitement, I relent and agree that he can get ready first and off he goes to shower.

I follow my nose to the kitchen and spot the plate of cookies cooling. They look like raisin, which is nice, but I was sure I could smell chocolate.

I glance around.

Hidden in a Tupperware, in Mikey's open duffel bag, is a big stack of chocolate cookies. I take two and replace them with the raisin ones to teach him a lesson for hiding them from me.

The cookies are delicious, bitter dark chocolate and perhaps a hint of ginger, whatever the ingredients, I love them so much I even inhale the crumbs from my palm.

***

At seven p.m. on the dot, Damien Watkins sounds the intercom to inform me that he has arrived to pick me up. I wouldn't normally agree to being picked up from home, but Melinda reassured me that he is a police officer and a salt of the earth type of fellow. She knows him personally and vouches for his character.

So far so good.

I opt for a classic little black dress with a high neckline and skyscraper heels to lengthen my legs. It also reveals an ample side of thigh, but since we will be sitting down for most of the evening, it seems a safe enough option.

I'm already feeling unusually positive about the evening as I strut down the corridor like a runway model. I realise I've been too down on men and life in general. I'm a confident, thirty-something woman who is in total control of her destiny. There are only good things ahead for me from now on.

When I reach the foyer, I'm not even alarmed to see Six, who looks like he's just finished at the gym in his little shorts and vest top, even though the weather is still cold with a chance of rain.

I smile sweetly. I'm a strong, confident woman after all.

"I still want my trombone, Four," Six warns.

I want to retaliate, to say something like, "You'll just have to blow on something else," but my mouth is suddenly so dry I can barely talk, so I ignore him and wave to my date, who is actually very good looking.

Damien has a 'boy-next-door' vibe going on. His hair is shiny and blonde with a slight kink to the edges. I splutter at the thought of the word 'kink,' causing Six to look at me and then to Damien.

Trust Six to be jealous.

The thought pleases me and I smirk. I take my longest strides to emphasise the wiggle of my butt as I sashay towards my date: Nice Damien, the police officer. Perhaps if I ask him nicely he can get me some of that crime scene tape to put around my car parking space. I decide I'll ask him for some.

Damien's car is red, like a cherry. He drives carefully and it feels like eleven hours before we get to the restaurant, but when I check my watch, it's only been ten minutes.

My stomach groans the whole way but Damien doesn't notice because I fill the time with impromptu giggles and random conversation. Suddenly, I want to know all about him, his family, his cat, his favourite colour. I start a conversation about whether rats or mice would be worse as guests at our table. He looks almost endeared by my descent into crazy and answers my odd line of questioning with a smile.

Damien parks outside the restaurant, a cosy red brick building just outside of town that advertises two-for-ones on main courses. It's the type of establishment families and groups of friends frequent because of its value for money and large portions, which really is fine by me.

The waiter looks to be about twelve years old and stares at my legs as we walk in. I'm not sure if it's because my legs look good or because I take out a stray toddler on the run from its parent.

"Oops," I say with a smile. "Isn't he cute. I like kids. They're so little and crazy. Would you like kids, Damien?"

Shit. Why did I say that?

"I mean not that I want them. I find them a bit weird to be honest. I couldn't eat a whole one." I snort a laugh.

When did I start snorting?

Damien smiles to placate me. I wonder if he is already regretting this date. The waiter points to a booth with red plastic benches and a chequered tablecloth.

Damien sits opposite me, instead of beside me, to keep a respectful distance I expect.

We order our food. Everything looks so delicious. I'm ravenous so I order a starter, a main course and two sides.

"You must be starving," he asks, his smile meets his brown eyes and I stare into them, mesmerized.

"Such nice eyes, just like chocolate," I say with a dreamy tone. "Oh no. Did I just actually say that aloud?" I laugh. I really laugh, and the couple at the table beside us raise their eyebrows and roll their eyes at me. I pick up the menu and hide my face, and snort like a five year old.

Damien's a gentleman and he hands me my wine when I start to choke. I try my best to stop with the giggles and am relieved when our food is finally served and I can calm my nervous stomach by stuffing it full of food.

Sated by food, I lean back in the chair and twiddle the ketchup bottle, which is shaped like a tomato. It really is lovely.

Damien studies me with a look of confusion. I bashfully smile and my face warms.

"You have a little…" Damien uses his index finger to point to the corner of his own mouth.

My mind catches up to the gesture and I begin to apologise. I'm not usually so uncouth, but instead I ungracefully burp in response. The smell of lemon and garlic and onion rings hangs in the air between us like an unwelcome neighbour.

"I'll be right back." I smile and excuse myself to the

bathroom.

I stumble but mostly manage to stay upright on the skyscraper heels. I nearly take out a waiter, but thankfully his reactions are quick and he holds me up while balancing a tray of drinks.

I can't work out what has gotten into me. I'm not normally so unstable. I start to wonder if Damien is as darling as Melinda suggested. What if he spiked my drink? You hear about it all the time, don't you? Young, single female goes on a date with a hot, trustworthy looking guy and turns up dead two weeks later in a park, naked and found by joggers.

I quicken my pace to the bathroom. I'm too young to be murdered; my life has barely just begun.

I knock a teenager out the way to take the last cubicle first and turf the contents of my clutch out on the seat of the toilet. I'll call the police. They can come rescue me, take a swab of my mouth or a urine sample and prove that he's corrupt.

Shit!

He is police; they're probably all corrupt. They'll find drugs in my system and I'll end up doing hard time. I'm too pretty to go to jail. Tears start to fall down my face and I search for my phone on the seat of the loo.

It starts to ring.

"Melinda? Oh, thank god. I'm trapped in the toilet. I think I'm on drugs and I might be about to be murdered. Melinda, I don't want to go to jail. Don't let him murder me." I cry real tears in the hope she'll speak to her friend, the police officer, and he won't kill me out of respect for their friendship.

"Joanie, you need to listen really carefully and answer all my questions, okay?" She says it slowly, perhaps she's with the police right now and they need this conversation to nail the murderer.

I nod profusely.

"Where are you?"

I describe the cubicle in such meticulous detail, my police officer friend outside would be proud.

"Okay, Joanie, now that we've ascertained what the toilet looks like and we know they need to clean the seat more thoroughly, let's hear which restaurant you are in."

As I reel off the name of the restaurant, panic rises up in me. I must be in real danger. I hear her repeat the address to someone in the background.

"Melinda, I feel funny and I'm scared," I tell her.

"Right Joanie, you're doing really well. Something happened tonight, something bad. But I don't want you to panic. Someone's on their way to get you."

Being told not to panic is like throwing gas on the flames. I move my stuff so I can sit on top of the loo seat and wait to hear this awful news.

"Joanie, did you take the cookies from Mikey's bag?" Melinda asks.

I nod. Yes I did. My thoughts don't quite catch up to her point.

"Don't panic but Mikey made some special pot cookies, and now, well now you're stoned off your nut having dinner with a police officer. But it's okay. Help is on the way."

I drop the phone and hold my head in my hands.

Pot, cookies, stoned, police officer.

Oh, I guess it all makes sense now. I pick up my phone as if it is my life source, and cry into it, "Melinda! I'm stoned."

"Yep."

"I'm having dinner with a police officer!"

"Uh-huh."

"Fuck! Melinda, I ordered a starter, two sides and a main course!"

"Standard issue stoner dinner, Hun."

"I ate all of Damien's onion rings!"

Melinda starts to laugh and it's catching. I slide off the toilet and onto the floor clutching my sides. My brain has eloped with my sanity, nothing makes sense but everything is hilarious.

"Melinda? I'm too pretty to go to jail," I say between gasps, as though vanity is a valid reason not to go to jail.

A deep male voice echoes into the female bathroom.

"Sorry, excuse me, let me through. Joanie?"

I stay hidden behind my cubicle door for protection, in case it is a trap.

"Melinda, someone's calling my name," I whisper.

"It's okay, I sent help to rescue you. You can open the door, help is at hand. I phoned Damien and told him you're not well and he's gone home now."

I cautiously open the door and am so relieved I jump into the arms of my saviour.

Trust Six to rescue me.

Chapter 10

My body is the weight of a prehistoric animal that's attempting to stretch and bring its heavy bones back to life.

I had the funniest dream. I was in the jungle trying to eat a dinosaur with a knife and fork—I'm not a savage, after all. It felt so real, like it was actually an achievable task. I chuckle to myself, realising I'm not in the jungle I'm safe at home, in my own bed with my fleecy, Chesney Hawks blanket wrapped around me. It's bliss.

I stretch and pull the comforter, to tug it up to my chin. It jolts but won't come closer.

Strange.

I manually open my right eye with my finger and thumb. There's a big person lying on my bed, weighing down my comforter. It makes a light snuffling sound when I prod the dark mop of hair that falls over the intruders face.

It's Six.

My eyes widen. Six is snuffling on my bed and stealing Chesney without a care in the world.

I lick at my finger, wipe away my eye-snot, and check

the odour of my dry mouth before Six awakens. My fears are confirmed, my breath smells as if I died last night.

"Hmmpff…" Six snuffles again.

I watch him. My dry mouth is making it almost impossible to swallow, but I lick my lips anyway.

What is Six doing in my bed?

I carefully check my clothes. I'm wearing my little black dress which has shrunk to a Barbie sized ensemble and now ends at my navel.

Please God, don't let Six have seen my Power Pants. The ones that neither sit inside nor outside of my derrière, meaning I have to discretely pick them out at regular intervals. The ones that I wear because they also keep any lumps and bumps to a minimum.

I quietly wrestle against the tightness of my dress, desperate not to wake Six, at least until my modesty is covered. Then, he's being shown the door.

My desperation to pee is in direct conflict with my desire to cover my ass. The tightness of my hold-me-in knickers only making matters worse. I'm sure I can hear Canadian waterfalls and London rivers as they gush.

It's no good. The material of my dress won't pull down unless I remove the blanket from its tangled state, and in doing so I risk waking Six. It's a risk I must take, peeing in the bed with Six would definitely be worse than him seeing my granny pants.

I carefully unravel Chesney from the twisted straight jacket that he has become, and pray the mattress doesn't squeak as I crawl off it.

When my feet touch ground, I chance a glance back. Six's T-shirt lays on the floor beside my bed. He's sleeping shirtless, reclining against my black faux leather headboard that in this light matches both the hair on his head and the fine smattering of hair between his square, hard pectoral muscles. He looks so good, like an Adonis male model resting between shots.

Trust Six not to get snotty-eye or garbage breath.

My phone is on my dresser. I'll have to be quick, or I really might pee on my floor. I open up the camera app, no need for a flattering filter today and take a quick snap. I make a fatal error.

What happens next is in slow motion.

The camera clicks in an audible snap. Six snuffles, and one eye, his right eye, opens in a flash.

"Four, did you just photograph me sleeping?" he asks. His voice is a husky, sleepy groan.

My arm is still outstretched, the incriminating device still clenched in my hand. I can't deny it, yet I can't explain it.

I am a pervert, I know.

As if paparazzi faced with a lawsuit, I run out of the bedroom and into my bathroom, locking the door behind me.

How do I get myself into these situations?

I hide my phone in the laundry hamper, pee and then shower. I'll just deny the photograph. He can't prove it after all. He was half asleep.

After my shower, I check my reflection in the mirror. My cheeks are flushed as if I spent the whole night having torrid sex.

Unable to employ any more delay tactics, I go face the music and to find out what Six is actually doing in my bed.

Six is no longer in my bedroom, so I dress quickly in skinny jeans and a sweater and follow the smell of coffee. Six sits at my dining table, a pot of coffee and two cups in front of him. He has put his T-shirt back on and sits with his feet on the chair opposite. I sit beside him and wait for the onslaught.

"How are you feeling?" he asks. His eyes have a soft kindness to them.

"I feel okay, a bit hung over. I remember bits of last night; flashes of information, really. I think I probably drank too much wine, you know, on top of the cookies." I flush with embarrassment. It feels like I am confessing to my Headmaster.

"Yes, Four. Not your finest moment." Six bites on his lip, to keep from laughing. His amusement of my situation is infuriating.

"What? Oh, you think this is my fault? That I knowingly eat pot cookies and go on dates with police officers for thrills? Well, Six, I'll have you know that if I wanted that kind of excitement then I'd just stay home and get tortured by you!" I huff and fold my arms in front of my chest, as if I am a petulant child.

"Now, now, Four. We're being nice, remember? I'm even going to let you keep the photograph you took of me…"

My mouth opens to deny his slanderous accusations but he interrupts. "We will never mention the shot again, if you forgive Mikey, no questions asked. He's feeling incredibly bad, so much so he's gone into hiding. Between you and me, he's staying at Melinda's place if you want to phone him and make up."

"Hiding? More likely he's still laughing!"

The corner of Six's mouth twitches and I know I am right.

"I could kill him, Six. I was on a date with a police officer!" I hold my face in my hands.

The sound of the coffee pouring into cups catches my attention and I look up. Six concentrates as he idly puts milk and sugar into both cups. He's fascinating to watch. His fingers are long and the muscles on his forearms are full and dense. I wish I wasn't in the naughty corner, so I could actually bare to meet his eyes with mine.

"You'll forgive him; he saved your ass in the end. He called Melinda to come rescue you, after he worked out you replaced his special cookies, with the raisin cookies. But she was stranded at her house with her kids. He thought he was the last person you would want to see once you knew, so he knocked on my door. It was interesting to watch your friends all concerned for your welfare. They care a lot about you, that's for sure."

"Is that so hard to believe?" I ask, my eyes meeting his, my curiosity getting the better of me.

He reaches his hand across the table; his fingers twist the heart on my charm bracelet. "No, Four, that's not hard to believe at all."

The beat of my heart spikes and thumps. I pick up my coffee with shaking hands needing a distraction from the intensity of his gaze. The coffee is too hot and it burns on the way down.

"Why did you stay?"

"Four, you don't seem the type of woman to get high normally, and Melinda was worried you might throw up in your sleep and choke, so I agreed to stay and make sure you didn't die."

"Until you fell asleep, you mean?" I smile at him and he raises a cocky eyebrow in return.

"Hey, you were in no condition to stay awake in your bed with me, Four. Had you been, I don't think either of us would have gotten any sleep."

I remember his Viking-like body, in only a pair of jeans and take another sip of coffee while I look away. Being utterly sleep deprived has never sounded so attractive.

"Is this a truce, then? Are we friends now?" I ask, changing the subject before I say something embarrassing.

"I don't think we'll ever be friends, Four," he replies.

My chin juts out and my eyes narrow. "Fine," I reply. "No skin off my nose."

"I meant… Never mind. Why do you continue to go on these silly dates anyway? Surely you're not so desperate?"

My anger flares. Who does Six think he is?

"No, I am not desperate!" I say incredulously, in shock at his cheek. "I am trying to meet someone. I am sick of…" being lonely, being with the wrong guy, "stupid men who think they know everything!" I glare at him.

Six's nostril's flare. "Well you are putting yourself in

danger, meeting a bunch of guys you don't even know. It's reckless!"

I stand and my hands grip the table.

"Oh, well you should know all about reckless, Six. After all, you nearly pummelled Twenty's head right through my wall! How is it fair that you, I mean, guys in general can screw whomever they like, but I go on a few blind dates and I'm reckless!" I yell.

His lips purse and he stands too.

"I never, I mean, Twenty has nothing to do with this, she's not even... You are putting yourself in danger. Who's the next guy, huh, Four? Ted Bundy? Maybe you'll strike it lucky and they won't murder you, they'll just keep you as a pet!"

Six starts to leave and I follow him, yelling like some kind of crazy banshee.

"Thanks for keeping me alive." I use finger punctuation to emphasise his ridiculousness. "But I think I'd rather take my chances. It's not like it can be any less risky than living next to you!"

"You keep telling yourself that, Four!"

Six opens the door and I slam it behind him.

Trust Six to have the last word!

***

Even though I mostly feel like cancelling today's date, I don't. Firstly, I don't want to give Six the satisfaction of thinking I've listened to his self-righteous advice; and secondly, it's paintballing, which I've always wanted to try. Shooting the shit out of something might be just the cure for my pent up aggression.

I dress as super-hot as possible—in old clothes that I don't mind ruining. I opt for black skinny jeans that lengthen my little legs and a blue lightly padded bomber jacket, which I pray provides me with some further protection. I tie my long hair in two cute long plaits and put on a baseball cap. Ready, I walk the four streets to get in my car and drive to the venue.

Date six is with Dominic Baldwin. Melinda's report explains that Dominic, thirty-five, and a Taurus is a divorced marine, with two children. Whilst a pre-made family wouldn't be my first choice, I consider Melinda's current predicament and decide it would be wholly unsavoury to blacklist him on the basis of kids. I love Melinda's kids as if they were my own family, and the thought of anyone ruling her out based on her adorable kids fills me with rage. So, I lead by example and go on a date with this man.

When I reach the clearing in the forest, date number six is standing exactly where he said he would, under the entrance sign.

I fan my face as he comes into view. He is tall and his shoulders are so broad he looks a perfect triangular shape, if not for his head. Which in truth, looks a little on the small side. He's dressed in full marine-chic, camouflage bottoms, tight black T-shirt and, yep, dog tags around his neck. He waves as I drive under the barrier and then hops in my car to give me directions.

He smells of grass (not that kind!) and dew. It's a rugged, all-terrain manly smell. For some reason, unknown to me, the more manly he behaves, like when he offers to park my car for me, the more girly and feminine I behave.

"So, Joanie, Melinda says great things about you," he says sporting real life dimples on his big square jaw. On closer inspection, his hair isn't just short, it's mostly thinning to the point he's shaved it army-issue short. "Have you been paintballing before?"

I explain that no, this is an extreme measure for me (the paintballing and the ten dates). My date informs me that he is very into extreme sports and that if I enjoy today, he could introduce me to bungee jumping, parachuting, and air soft. I nod, though in all honesty I'm not sure any of that sounds very appealing.

I'm given some overalls to wear over my own clothes, which I put on in the clearing, while my date goes to use the bathroom.

I huddle with the others, bouncing on the spot to keep warm against the icy breeze. The cruddy ground is frozen solid and I wonder if I fell, rather than providing a cushion, the jewel-like moss would cut like ice. I start to wonder if paintballing in January was a good idea.

When a long whistle is blown, the park ranger, a burly man in his fifties with the look of a sergeant major, orders us to sit in a horseshoe shape on some fallen trees, where he starts to yell his talk. It's mostly rule based about not shooting members of the same team or the staff, and then he moves on to how we'll only play four games this afternoon and be all done by four p.m. since it'll be getting dark by then.

When he's finished yelling, the ranger moves around the attendees and ticks off everyone's name from his register. When he gets to me, I scratch my head as I start to panic. I can't remember my date's name. I discretely lean to my right, to try and crane my neck to see the names, hoping for a spark of recognition. The ranger eyes me suspiciously and moves his clipboard out of reach.

I'm not a person who thinks well under stress, but even I am impressed by my quick thinking genius. I put my palms up, my eyebrows rise with them, though it's not strictly necessary, and I say, "Non Anglais, monsieur."

I have no idea if my French is as good as the low-grade pass I earned at school, but the ranger nods eagerly; probably glad I'm not a complete fool. He thinks I just couldn't understand what he was saying.

"Ah," he knowingly nods once again, smacking his thigh and offering me an enthusiastic ear-to-ear grin. He certainly seems pleased that I can't understand him. "Comment tu t'appelles?" he says.

It's so cold I can't feel my feet, but I can feel my cheeks, which are suddenly on fire. My brain takes a while to operate the search and find function, but when it does, I jump up from the log as if I just won the lotto.

"Je m'appelle Joanie." I smile, totally nailing the French language.

The ranger nods excitedly, someone took an evening class in French and suddenly can't wait to use it. Fear flares my fight or flight mode. I start hopping and look around totally missing whatever French the ranger throws back at me. I spot the bathroom in the distance. In a display of sheer desperation, but not that kind—I hold my crotch and bob up and down—the ranger gives me a thumbs up, says something else in French and then thumbs the direction.

I run towards the bathroom.

I'm going to have to avoid the ranger from here on out.

After leaving the bathroom, I hide in some foliage while the ranger stands with my date and ticks off our names from his clipboard. Once the ranger walks away, I cautiously close in on my date.

My nerves start to get the better of me as my date hands me my helmet and rifle as we approach our first battle. He gingerly asks me why the ranger thinks I can't speak English. I feign a non-committal answer, explaining that he's probably gone a bit weird, spending all this time in the woods. My date nods understanding, as though my suggestion is at least plausible.

I wonder if I'm about to get hurt. My earlier G.I. Jane bravado has long since evaporated. Maybe, if I just stick with this military trained man who's most likely an experienced fighter, I can survive this.

We follow the group to an old, dilapidated bus with no seats that sits in the middle of the clearing. Sensing my nerves, my date wraps his arm around my shoulder as we're given our objective—defend the flag sticking out from the front of the bus.

I steel myself to be brave.

The ranger wishes me luck in English but with a

French accent. My date eyes him like the strange man that he thinks he is.

My team splits up, taking either end of the bus and spots behind trees. When I look around, my date is rubbing dirt from the ground onto his cheeks. I consider what good hands I am in, no need to be scared; this man is a trained professional. Then—and I can't believe that he does this—my date, sprints into the woods without so much as a backward glance.

I start to hear gunfire and shouts as people are shot. My heart thumps from my chest and I can no longer feel the cold, only the beating of my heart. I need to run, if I am to survive this. I look to the direction of my date. I can make it; I know I can. I hitch my gun in front of my face and start to jog. Suddenly, there's an explosion and chaos ensues. Fog, in a haze of pinks, lilacs, and purples, cloud my vision. I'm blind, I can't even see the bus. I can't see my salvation, and I can't see the enemy. My breathing is ragged heaves and shallow breaths. I'm hyperventilating, and then something terrible happens.

First, my left calf, as if bit by a dog, is hit so hard it's taken out from underneath me. I hit the cold hard ground with a thud that causes the cheeks of my ass to smart. It's then that I am shot. Repeatedly. My shoulder, back and arms, every inch of my torso feels lashed, beaten and raw. I try to hold my gun in the air like they told me. I yell at the top of my lungs and then, well then, I pass out from pain   and   trauma.

Chapter 11

Our teaching hospital, Saint Jude's, is full of young, fit, virile doctors that are keen to advance their knowledge and demonstrate the very best of bedside etiquette.

After arriving by ambulance, standard procedure apparently when one cannot weight bear, the handsome doctor gives me a thorough work up. He even introduced me to several of his doctor friends so they can inspect my injury, which is not due to the painful lacerations and bruising from the paintballs. No, it was simply not good enough for me to be stretchered from the battlefield with cuts and bruises, a badly damaged ego and crying tears so real that even baby Annabelle would be envious.

No, not Joanie Fox.

The doctor, a young looking Clark Kent, looks at his chart and proceeds with his evaluation. "So, Miss Fox, we've X-rayed for pelvic fracture, the results of which are negative. We've run the blood samples that you insisted on, following that episode of Greys Anatomy you watched that one time, and I'm pleased to say there are no markers for any kinds of tumours despite the achy leg you had earlier."

Melinda holds my hand from the seat beside my bed reassuringly. My date had called her to meet me at the hospital, apparently preferring to stay and fight for my honour.

The doctor continues, "You have…" his eyes skim the clipboard. His colleague beside him looks to double check. They nod their heads at one another as I prepare myself for bad news. "You have a Buttock Contusion."

When I gasp and clench Melinda's hand a little harder, he continues, "In short, it's a bruising to the rear. It may cause some residual swelling in the short-term, but there's no need for the private room you asked for earlier. I am happy to say that your injury will completely heal during the next week to ten days."

The doctor gives Melinda an information leaflet about lying on my side, treating the injury with ice, heat, massage, and over-the-counter pain relief.

"It's just a bruise?" I ask, not sure whether I ought to ask for a second opinion. It is so painful I can barely walk and that's after the pain relief the doctor has given me.

I hold my head in my hands.

Trust Four to go on a date and come home with an embarrassing ass injury.

***

Melinda pulls her car up as close to my building as possible, and I lean on her shoulder as she assists me into the foyer. I can tell that I am testing her patience by her hardened jaw and well-timed hisses; patience is not a well-practiced skill for Melinda.

She takes my key and opens the foyer door with one hand, while supporting my weight with the other. Every step and movement provokes me to gasp and beg for a rest.

"Four, are you okay? You're as white as a sheet."

I try to seek out the noise that comes from behind me,

even though I know it is Six.

Melinda's response beats mine. "She has a pain in her ass and will likely be closed for business for a while."

"Well, she's been a pain in my ass for a while now. Seems only fitting the shoe slides to the other foot." Six follows his comments with his cocky grin as he comes into view and appraises me with those dark navy eyes of his.

Melinda chuckles in a friendly, open manner and then asks, "And you are?"

"Six. Pleasure to meet you."

Melinda's eyebrows shoot up like fireworks. She traitorously smiles at Six as she shakes his hand, ignoring the fact that I'm just inches from them both.

"Of course you are. Nice to meet you, Six. She didn't mention you were so… tall."

I close my eyes. My devastation consumes me. Melinda continues, "You wouldn't give me a lift with this one would you? She's heavier than she looks."

"Is she?" I ask. Neither of them notices the shaking of my head or the look of death I fire from my eyes.

"It would be my pleasure."

Six hoists me up carefully onto his shoulder, into a lift that stirs a vivid memory from deep inside of me. I let out a gasp as pain shoots in my butt. Six carries my weight with little effort, and we quickly reach the door of my apartment.

Even if I wanted to protest, I can't. The slightest of movements cause shooting white-hot pain in my butt. I hold my breath while Melinda opens my door and Six walks inside and lowers me gently onto my side on the sofa.

"Shall I make us some tea?" Melinda offers.

I decline. I'm not sure I could stay awake for the length of time it takes for the kettle to boil. Melinda goes into the kitchen anyway and returns with an ice pack that she lies across my butt.

Sleep takes me hard and fast. But, in the gap before I

fall, a small part of me hopes that when I wake, Six is still here to look after me.

***

The first thing I notice when I wake is that my ass still throbs with pain, so much so I don't dare move. The second thing I notice is Six seated on the chair opposite my sofa. He doesn't notice I'm awake, he's reading the medical leaflet I was given at the hospital. His bare feet are on my coffee table and he's wearing light jeans with rips at the knees. They look so good I question how I missed them earlier. I allow my eyes to drift, just for a moment, while he is entertained. I am sure he will ridicule me later but his body is so ripped it would be rude not to look while I can. His white T-shirt clings to his chest and looks soft enough to wrap babies in. I wonder what our babies might look like.

Six looks at me strangely, I close my mouth and offer him a friendly smile.

"Good evening, Four. Your friend Melinda asked me to stay; she had to get back to her kids," Six says.

It's dark outside. The clock says ten. Six has shut the curtains and put on the lamp. He's even draped me in Chesney, and I'm still lying on my side but the icepack from earlier is gone.

"Thank you, for staying again."

"Where else would I be," Six murmurs. "Mikey dropped in some freshly made soup and bread. Would you like me to heat you some?"

I nod, suddenly ravenous.

A funny feeling flutters through my belly when Six, in his bare feet, takes ownership of my kitchen. He heats the soup and brings me the bowl with three chunks of freshly baked bread. I watch him clean the kitchen while I eat and think back to how Chris looked in the same kitchen not two weeks ago. My stomach doesn't feel as fluttery, so I concentrate on my soup which is divine.

Six brings us both tea and sits opposite me, back in his chair, with his feet once again on the coffee table. I wonder if he'll make his excuses to go home soon, now that he doesn't have a reason to stay.

Six takes the television remote from the coffee table and pushes the on button. He catches me looking and throws me a grin. "What?" he says innocently.

"Nothing," I reply, surprised by his sudden civility. In reverse, I'd probably be tempted to tease.

The television blinks on and Six changes the channel. Then he looks away from the television and focuses on me. His smile parts to reveal his teeth. "Can I ass you a question?"

Six's abdominal muscles bob with his silent laugh.

"Spit it out Six; get it all out your system now. But be warned, when I am not in so much pain, I will get you back," I threaten.

"Fair comment, I'm sorry, Four. Is there anything I can do to ass-ist you?" Six's silent laugh increases to a barely audible chuckle. "Perhaps I can get you some Ass-pirin?"

"Hilarious, Six." I shake my head and narrow my eyes, fighting the grin that wants to break free.

"Sorry, I'm putting all my jokes ass-ide; you have my ass-urances." His laugh leaves his lips in unrestrained chugs until he gives up and belly laughs. Six's face when he smiles like this is such a treat for sore eyes I don't even have it in me to be offended.

"You're an ass-hole, you know that, Six?" I crack up at the sight of Six laughing and at my own humiliation, but the movement my body makes, as my belly laughs creases me up, causing me to shriek with pain.

Six leaps up and perches next to me.

"It says massage is helpful." He points to the leaflet, a glint of concern in his eyes. His hand goes to the painful swell of my right buttock. He looks at me for permission. I pretend I don't see him and sigh as he rubs at the tight, hard muscle. It's a glorious, deep rub and my eyes flutter and blink in euphoric release.

After a few minutes, he moves from his awkward position in front of the sofa and carefully lifts my feet onto his lap. As he sits beside me, he continues his massage and we settle to watch the film playing on the television.

***

The light streams through the curtain and I wipe the sleep dust from my eyes. Six snuffles his light snores from the end of the sofa, and I uncomfortably try to shift my body. The pain shoots like a rocket through my butt cheek and my leg jolts out like fork lightening.

Six lurches up off the sofa, cupping his man parts. "Jesus, Four, you nearly disabled the crown jewels, again."

"Oops. Sorry, Six." He gives his balls the lightest of fondles. Confident there is no damage, he moves to the kitchen and I hear the kettle switch on.

While he is busy, I take one of the stainless steel coasters from my coffee table and inspect my morning look. My face is pale and dark circles haunt my eyes. There's a smattering of dirt with essence of green paint. I'm still wearing my paintball clothes, minus my jacket and my Bon Jovi T-shirt has rips and stains. The effort to lift my arms so I can sniff my pits is excruciating, and I let out a groan as my tender joints stretch.

I need a shower, but I know it's going to hurt, bad. I use both hands to heave myself off the sofa, crying out as I do. Six is suddenly at my side, his hand under my arm. Water leaks from my eyes, and I start to wonder how I am going to manage to walk into the bathroom, never mind actually shower. Six seems to understand my predicament. He puts his arms beneath mine and supports my weight as we walk together, where he leaves me in the bathroom.

I'm able to undo my zip and relieve myself. I manage to switch on the shower and kick off my trousers with great difficulty. Every slight movement feels like I'm lifting the weight of ten men. I wretch with pain and shock when I see my butt protruding from my underwear. If this was a police line-up of butts, then mine could be mistaken for a Kardashian's, either that or two hard purple footballs.

"Four, are you okay? Open the door." My T-shirt barely covers my navel and I'm in a state of disrepair. My body is black, blue, purple, and green. Parts of the shot wounds are bright red welts of raw skin and sting as the air touches them.

It's no good; I will need to stay dirty and smelly.

I sob and reply to Six, "I can't do this. It hurts too much. I can't even lift my arms to take my top off."

"Four, I'm coming in," he says, knocking twice for good measure and opening the door.

I let out a snigger, which hurts like hell, but the consequential pain is worth it when I notice what Six is wearing. "Six, is that my bra?"

"It was on the radiator in the kitchen; it looked about the right size."

Six is wearing my off-white sports bra as a curtain across his eyes. My heart does a little flip. He looks so vulnerable and sweet, blindfolded by my bra.

"Right, I'm here to help. Just tell me where not to grab."

I stand in front of Six and move his hands to the hem of my shirt. "Take it off real slow," I tell him and he lifts it and releases my arms in lingering, careful movements. I turn my back to him and ask him to undo my bra. He carefully feels his way to the clasp and unhooks it. My breasts, released from their prison feel as though they engorge in size, and I consider what a shame it is that he can't see them. Six slides the straps down from my shoulders, his long fingers are light and create a path of goose bumps in their wake. I guide his hands to my hips, and audibly swallow the lump as he slides my underwear down over my curves to the floor. My pain is like a distant memory, as parts of my body heat with pleasure, until I shift my weight to stand closer to the bathtub.

"Ahh," I let out a sigh, and Six is suddenly quite literally standing to attention in front of me.

"Grab hold of me if you need to, Four. We've got this," Six says, and I can't help but admire his erection, though I'm not sure that was what he was referring to me grabbing. I grip his arm, I'm a lady after all, and he feels across my back and supports under my arms while I climb over the side of the bath and under the warm jets.

I groan in pleasure at the sensation of the warm water as I watch Six, standing guard. I could pull the shower curtain across, but amazingly, I trust that he won't peek. It would be erotic if everything weren't so damned painful. I lather myself up using my cherry scented body wash and begin to feel more like a woman again.

Six's nostril's flare as he inhales, the water spraying him slightly. The bulge in his area seems to have swollen even more, and I'm questioning the strength of the denim from releasing his beast. I'm drenched, and not because of the shower.

"Do you need me to do anything, Four?"

Oh my, is he...

"I could wash your hair if you need me to, just pour the soap in my hands." He holds out his hands in cups.

Urghh. Trust Six to suddenly become a gentleman.

I pour the shampoo into his waiting hands and he asks me to say when his hands are above my scalp. He performs a massage capable of bankrupting salons across the land. Groans escape my mouth, which, judging by the look on Six's face pleases him greatly. While he rinses the suds from my hair, his T-shirt becomes soaked and I admire his firm chest and solid muscles as he works me—I mean my hair—into a frenzy. Too soon, the soap is all rinsed out, but I decide I need conditioner. It's better to be thorough. Six's T-shirt is now soaking wet. He asks me to hang on while he removes it. I tell him it's a good idea, I don't want him to get cold, after all.

He removes it slowly and carefully, so not to remove the blindfold. It's an erotic striptease.

A shirtless Six is a sizzling sight.

I wonder if it'd be crass to suggest the conditioner ought to soak in for five minutes, so that I can admire the view, but Six proceeds with the rinsing, and since his fingers are moving in my hair and his elbow accidentally brushes my nipple, the thought is soon washed clean.

When I can't prolong the shower any longer, Six grabs my fluffiest towel from the radiator, and wraps it around me, tucking it in at the side of my breast.

I'm left breathless and throbbing, and not because of my injuries.

Trust Six to make getting clean absolutely filthy.

Chapter 12

After I am dressed and Six has helped me put on my socks and settle back onto my side on the sofa, he nips next door for another T-shirt. Six returns after only a minute or two with his toolbox and some breakfast ingredients. He makes us bacon and eggs, even though it is nearing lunchtime, and he serves it with coffee so strong you could eat it with a spoon.

"You know, Four, you buy really terrible coffee. It tastes like cat's pee." Six stocks his coffee in my canister. I don't complain. I quite like Six's coffee, now that I'm used to it.

After we have eaten, Six washes the dishes and fixes a broken cupboard handle in the kitchen. He complains that I have my heating switched up too high. I'm tempted to suggest that if he's too warm he could take off his T-shirt again, but leave the tool belt on...

My mind wanders into dark, delicious places. I don't

recall a time before now that I have ever fantasized over a man. My filthy little imagination is more than compensating for this fact. I realise, for the first time that I could totally get used to having Six around. Especially since, for the last few hours, he has hardly been annoying at all. Perhaps we have turned a corner in our relationship

Six sits opposite me in his chair. His feet, minus socks, are resting on my coffee table, again. I'm surprised that this doesn't annoy me since I used to make Chris wear slippers in the apartment; although, his feet were bony with wiry black hairs on his toes. Six's toes are tanned and smooth with short, clipped toenails. I'm not a person who normally notices feet, but it has to be noted that Six's feet are not offensive to the eye. Strangely, I like seeing him relax in my home.

Six clears his throat, catching my attention. When my gaze meets his, his eyebrows raise with his smile. "Something interesting about my feet?" he asks.

"Not at all," I tell him. I can't exactly admit I was just admiring his feet; that would be weird. "Actually, I'm just wondering if the painkillers are mellowing my mood." I throw a pointed eye at his offending feet, even though I don't really mind all that much.

"Do you want me to remove my feet, Four?" he asks.

"God, no! That would just make a mess; there'd be blood everywhere. Last time I made someone do that it took weeks to get the metallic smell out of the room," I mumble. Six's eyebrows rise up in that cute way when he finds something amusing, and he nods his understanding. He has a cheeky little smile on his lips as if he thinks I'm not completely mental. I change the subject. "Can you pass me my laptop, please?"

I point to the side of Six's chair and he carefully takes my laptop out from the bag and passes it to me. He then settles back in his chair, feet on the coffee table, to read the action book he must have brought from next door.

While we were at the hospital, Melinda called work to

explain that I am sick, but I need to email in some files I've been working on from home.

Once my laptop has whirled back to life, a familiar ringing echoes around the room. I answer the video call instinctively before I fully think through the repercussions. It will be my mother, who is the only person, apart from Melinda, to have ever video called me.

"There you are, my little brave soldier. I've been trying to contact you. Where is your phone? Melinda told me everything. How are you and how on earth do you manage to break your bottom, my dear girl?" My mum's words bluster out through the speakers.

Heat flares in my face as I angle the screen of my laptop away from Six, who puts his book down and studies my situation with interest. My fingers twitch nervously while trying to switch the volume down. My mum has a tendency to spill whatever lunacy pops into her head with no thought of consequence. She could literally give Six enough taunts, in just one sentence, to last a dozen years. I cuss myself for not having asked Six to pass me my earphones.

My mum is wearing rollers in her yellow hair and her perma-tanned face looks older than the last time we spoke. Her bright pink lipstick matches her shirt, which dips to reveal quite a bit of cleavage.

Six stands and I wonder if he is about to go home, to give me some privacy and leave me with my dignity intact.

"Oh, I have got to see this," he says and walks around the coffee table, leaning on the sofa behind me.

I give him my narrowed 'buzz off' glare and try to swat him away, but my mum sees him and leans her face forward until she's filling the screen of my laptop.

"Joanie, don't be alarmed but there is a man behind you and it isn't Chris!" She whispers this as if Six can't hear her just as clearly as I can.

I take a deep breath and try to steel myself for the embarrassment that's too late to avoid. "Mum, this is my neighbour. He's fixed my cupboard and has been helping me out, you know since I…"

"Broke your bum?" My mother fills in the gaps, just as she always does.

"Hurt myself," I clarify, while my mother and Six both examine me under their microscopes. "Chris and I, we um… broke up." I brace myself for her reaction. She loves Chris and was hoping for a shotgun wedding any day now. She said as much to anyone who cared to listen. "We um… Just wanted different things but I'm okay. It was for the best, really it was. He's gone to New York…" I shake my head to dispel my discomfort at this conversation. My back twinges and I try to rub at my tightening injuries.

I can still feel Six watching me; it makes me want to pull Chesney over my head. He climbs over the back of the sofa and slides my feet up onto his lap, pulling my Chesney blanket over our legs.

"Oh no, Joanie, my darling. Maybe he'll take you back. I could phone him, make him realise what a good girl you are. Maybe if you wear the push-up bra I bought you, with those nice shoes I sent you… You could send him some pictures of yourself to remind him what he's missing. Your father always preferred a busty woman, that's why I had the implants. Perhaps we could get you some for Christmas?"

My palms are sweating too much to press the key to end the call. Trust my mother to point out my shortcomings in the sexy underwear and breast department to Six!

I hold my head in my hands and take deep breaths. It will not do to lose my patience with my mother, she'll just think she's on to something and call Chris anyway. It'll be my senior prom all over again, when Robert Pearce's mother colluded with mine and we spent a painful three hours in each other's company.

I use the calm voice, an imitation of the one Melinda uses with her children—when I know she actually wants to lose her shit—as I tell my mum, "I'm not sure some saucy shots of me in sexy underwear and a boob job are really going to help…"

Six grabs the laptop from me. His eyes are dark and intense as he looks closely at my face. He can definitely see my mortification, which is probably why my body feels like it's breaking out in hives.

"Mrs.…?" Six turns the screen so that his face fills the box in the top right of the screen.

My mum's eyes widen and she manually heaves her bosom up for the camera. My mouth falls open and I call out, "Mum…" However, Six's hand gently cups my mouth to shh me.

"Fox, darling. But you can call me Beryl."

My mum flirts her ass off with Six as she explains that she had me young, even though we only look like sisters. If I wasn't agonized by pain before, I'm positively dying now.

"Mrs. Fox. Your daughter dumped her boyfriend because he was disrespectful and untrustworthy. She really is better off without him and please, believe me when I say this, Joanie really doesn't need breast implants. From what I can see, she has a perfectly perky set of breasts. They really are quite magnificent, in my humble opinion. She is, however, in a lot of pain, and I do think she should rest. It is absolutely a pleasure to meet you, though, Mrs. Fox and I promise to take good care of Joanie while she recovers."

Six gives my mum his trademark grin and my mum thanks him in return. She tells him that he should join me when I visit at Easter, that he could strip down to his shorts and enjoy the sunshine. Six then removes his hand from my mouth and passes me back my laptop, while my now released mouth falls open in spectacular cartoon style.

Six said my name.

Six just said my breast were 'perfectly perky.'

Six said my breasts were 'magnificent.'

I remove the dopey smile from my face, aware that Six can probably see the effect of his words and glance down to check. As if to confirm their approval of his description, my nipples ping to attention. I look at Six, who nods and gives them a thumb up.

The room is suddenly too warm, and I fan myself and shake my head at this strange turn of events.

"Joanie my darling, swan duck. I'm sorry, of course you can do without that Chris boy. I did always think he was a little too serious, a bit straight laced. Personally, I prefer a little more kink. Nevertheless, if you decide on the breasts, let them be our gift to you. I've never looked back since I got mine nor had so many men stop and stare." My mother winks, probably not even noticing the cringed look upon my face. "Now, tell me all about this handsome neighbour. He is a dish! How long have you been screwing him, and is he any good?"

Even though she cannot see him, my mother must be able to hear Six chuckling at my side as his hand idly squeezes my thigh and massages my ache.

"Mum, I really have to go. We'll speak later. I love you lots." I hang up before any more dangerous words can leave my mother's mouth.

"So, your mum's hot and a little bonkers. I can see where you get it from, Joanie." Six winks and cocks his head. I shake my head and close my eyes.

Trust Six to say my name like it's coated in chocolate and rolled in nuts.

***

Six's hand slides under the cover and up the leg of my shorts as he kneels over me. One hundred and eighty pounds of ripped, hard muscle with a side of soft dark hair that I can't wait to drag my fingers through hovers just inches above me. His eyes are solid black and hungry as he breathes my name into my mouth.

"Joanie, I want you."

I swallow hard. His breath is a mint-coffee ice cream,

cool and teasing on my neck as he moves to tell me, "I need you."

"I need you too," I say gripping his shoulder and closing my eyes as I part my lips in preparation for his kiss.

"Joanie, you're dribbling again…"

What?

He gently shakes my shoulder and tells me, "Joanie, you're needed."

"What?" I open my eyes and wipe my mouth with the back of my hand. He's right, definite case of the drools.

"You fell asleep. I think you were dreaming. You said my name. It was kind of cute, if I'm honest."

Six looks over from the other end of the sofa, snuggled under Chesney with my legs across his lap. He looks like he just woke up too; there's pillow creases marking the olive skin of his cheek.

I shake my dirty dream and the need to smooth his cheek from my mind and instead ask, "You said I was needed?"

"Your video calling has been ringing."

I wearily try to stretch out my leg and butt, which feels like it's seized up and been replaced by rusty iron. I look over at the still open laptop resting on the coffee table. It starts to bleep a ring again.

"Someone called Wayne apparently really wants to talk to you," Six says, wearing a look on his face that I don't recognise. Not his usual cocky smirk, sarcastic frown, or sexy smile; it's darker, like he's angry.

"Who's Wayne?" I ask, as if Six would know.

It starts to bleep and ring again. Six picks up the laptop and places it on my lap. "Why don't you answer it and see."

I gulp. I don't like the cross tone in his voice.

Beep, beep, beep…

Six taps a key and the call connects. A man suddenly blinks to life on my screen. Mid-thirties, five o-clock scruff stretched over a looking hard jaw. I can just see the neck muscles that stretch out to his shoulders. I look over at Six, not sure what's going on because I'm still feeling half-asleep.

"Uh, hello…" An unfamiliar deep voice fills my lounge.

Six's eyes snap to the screen of my laptop causing me to gulp like a naughty teenager, even though I have no idea why I feel so guilty.

"Hello…" I reply, still unsure what is going on.

"Joanie? Hi, I'm Wayne, Melinda's friend. She said she texted you and that you'd be expecting me to call for a Skype date. I'm working in Iceland, not back until the end of the month. She said you'd hurt yourself and would enjoy a little online date, which suits me. Is now a good time?"

I look at Six; his face is hard with a visible tick in his jaw. He studies me with such intensity it makes me so self-conscious I adjust my hair.

"So, I'm Wayne. I work on an oil rig, deep sea diving. Joanie, I go pretty deep and I can hold my breath for over two minutes." Wayne chuckles, clearly thinking he's funny. He's not. Six is funny, though. Six is strong too and carries me as if I'm light as air, and kisses me as though our lives depend on it. In fact, I'd bet Six could go pretty deep too. My hand clamps over my mouth, afraid I might have said my thought aloud.

I cringe.

I'm having date number seven while having dirty thoughts of Six, who's sitting right beside me. They say seven is supposed to be lucky, but this date feels like the worst luck in the whole world.

I stroke away the frown on my face.

Wayne continues, but all I see is Six's jaw tick from the corner of my eye. I can feel the heat and tension radiating from his body.

"I wish I could see you, Joanie. Can you stand, so I can look at you? Melinda said you're super hot, and I can tell she's not wrong. Move your hand down a little, so I can see you."

God this is awkward. I move my hand from my mouth. It rests on my heart, which is thumping out of my chest at an alarming rate. I'm about to say thank you, but now is not a good time for a video date. I'm not sure there will ever be a good time.

Wayne nibbles on his lip and his hand moves under the desk in front of him.

Before I get the chance to say that I'm cancelling our date, he continues, "Good girl, that's it move your hand. Lower; lift up your top; let me see you touch yourself. God, I'm getting hard just…"

My head pops back from the screen as my mind catches up to what Wayne's dirty little game is.

Six grabs the laptop and forces it shut, slamming it on the coffee table. He swings my legs carefully but swiftly aside and stands, then paces.

"Do you even realise the danger you are putting yourself in? Do you even know who any of these losers are, Four? When are you going to quit this stupid dating game? Wayne the Wanker just video booty called you!"

"I didn't… Lots of people go on blind dates. I wasn't expecting the video call. My phone is…" Still in hiding thanks to my indecent camera skills… "Never mind that. How the hell was I supposed to know he was going to video call me?" The tone of my voice increases by quite a few octaves. I'm angry that he's blaming me. "It's not as if I planned this. Melinda insisted on the dates and they've all been terrible, but what am I to do? I don't want to spend the rest of my life alone. I don't even like cats, Six! The last thing in the world I wanted was to be woken from that dream, by Wayne the Weirdo!"

"What dream?" Six stops pacing and his head twists to study my face, which floods with heat.

I study the paintball wound on my wrist, unable to make eye contact and wondering what to say to him that doesn't involve recalling my sexy little dream.

Six's face comes closer to mine, the heat of his breath sends shivers down my neck and a surge of heat to other, harder to reach places. Six lifts my chin so my eyes meet his. My heart hammers in my chest as he asks me again, "What dream?"

My thoughts jumble around inside my head, distracted by his presence. All I see is his beauty, all I feel is the intense range of emotions I have for him. The feeling of wanting to push him away, yet also wishing I could wrap myself around him is driving me insane.

He comes closer, waiting for my answer. He's so close, just inches from my mouth as he continues to wait. His close proximity fogs my brain and my words are incoherent as they slip from my lips.

"You, kissing... hard..."

Six must understand my description because he crushes his mouth on mine. His lips are soft yet firm against my own, parting my lips and his tongue deliciously staging a search and rescue from within my own mouth. My tongue willingly surrenders and we engage in the hottest of all slow dances.

Six's hand moves from my chin up into my hair, while he supports his weight with his other hand. My own hands ball in his T-shirt, so much so, I barely register my intent until I am pulling his T-shirt over his head and flinging it on the floor. As we are broken away from the intensity of our kiss, for just a moment, my eyes are torn between his mesmerizing body and the lure of his mouth. Six pulls me back in to taste my lips and unable to resist, I comply with enthusiasm. My fingers are frantic and frenzied on his arms, shoulders, and then his chest. They glide down to his abs and the valleys beside them, guiding my hands toward the Promised Land.

Six's hands slowly wander down to the hem of my shirt, distracting me from the task about to be in hand. Every inch of my body has suddenly come alive and demands his attention as his thumb skims my waist and moves to my navel. The feeling is so achingly good, I groan begging for more and lean up into his reach. Six responds to my request and hooks his hands underneath my knees, flipping my legs around him, readying us both for action, which… is a fatal, catastrophic error.

"AAOOOWWEEEEEE…" The howl rips through me like an animal seconds before it becomes road kill.

The muscles in my ass clench and retract, as if pummelled by a wrecking ball, the second my broken ass meets the fabric of the sofa.

"Shit! Sorry, Four I forgot." Six holds me under my arms, his face examining mine. The pain is so acute I feel like I might actually pass out. "Dammit, you've gone pale again. The blood has drained right out from your face."

I can't breathe. It hurts so bad I feel like I might actually pee. Six lowers me down gently as I arch my body so I don't sit directly on my broken ass. When I'm finally able to breathe, Six sits opposite me, back in his chair.

"So, I guess we're thinking third time lucky?" he says crossing his fingers. "Can I get you anything? Some pain relief, maybe?"

"No, I'm fine," I say, mourning my stolen orgasm.

Chapter 13

Six and I relax into the afternoon. He nipped out for a while to check on his business and came back with some soup. The whole time my body throbbed for release. I actually felt like a bomb ready to detonate. So much so that when a train went past the house earlier, it almost rocked more than my building.

Six serves me the soup. When he bends to put it on my lap, the desire to bite his tight, muscular ass almost takes over me. I'm twitchy and irritable and I know there is only one thing that will help. Well, two things, but one is sitting in a box under my bed and the other is walking around my apartment like a barefoot male model.

Dignity, Joanie. Remember your dignity.

After he's cleaned up, he brings me coffee and I complain I'm bored. More horny than bored, but I decide it's probably safer to tell him I'm bored.

"I bought you something," Six says, and hands me some magazines. He then relaxes back in his chair, socks off and feet on the coffee table about to read his book.

"Seriously? Urghh. I'm going to go crazy after a week of this!" I ungratefully whine.

"You know, Four, you are a terrible patient. Read, it'll help take your mind off… things." Six shifts uncomfortably in his chair and it dawns on me he probably has blue balls too. The thought revives my earlier yearning and a cruel throbbing intensifies, and I'm not referring to the one in my butt.

I huff and randomly open the magazine. It falls on the crossword page. I take the pen from the side table and chew on it as I consider my next move.

"Hmm. Six across, male ejaculation. Any ideas?" I ask innocently.

Six almost drops his book and looks at me quizzically. "Have you tried semen?" he asks.

"I'd love to…" I pause and a grin toys on my lips. "But it's too many letters…"

"Come?"

Yes please.

"That might work," I say. I put the pen in my mouth, purely for effect. I hear Six swallow and I smile. Six lifts his coffee to his lips. His dark eyes fixed on mine.

"Seven down, an intense feeling. Starts with an O?"

Six almost spits his coffee. He covers his surprise with a manly, hand over mouth cough and rests his cup back on the table.

"I know what you're doing. You, Four are a tease and you're torturing me. I'm looking forward to torturing you right back, once you're healed. I think I'll probably start by spanking you to teach you a lesson. This time, I think I'll make you wear the blindfold." His eyebrows arch and heat explodes inside of me like a flare. Six grins as if he knows he's hitting the spot. "Let's move on to safer ground, huh? Let's get to know one another, me first."

I nod. Second to touching more of Six is my desire to know more.

"That bloke I saw you in the foyer with, was that your ex?"

"Yes. That was Chris. He's gone to New York to

develop and re-launch his app, Sexy—Talk—Dating. You might have heard of it?" I say dismissively, hardly anyone has heard of it.

"Sexy—Talk—Dating? He called his app Sexy—Talk—Dating?" Six laughs and out of sheer habit I start to defend it by saying; it is a difficult market to break…

"S.T.D!" Six howls with laughter, clutching his sides and laying back in the chair.

"Oh my God. S.T.D!" How did I never realise. I cry with laughter, despite the pain it creates. We both giggle and snort as whole minutes pass by. "I can't believe I never saw that!" As our laughs pitter out and we dry our faces, I add, "I think I knew he wasn't the guy for me, you know, you get stuck in these situations and they roll on." I dismiss the woe me and make good on Six's promise to get to know each other. "My turn, what brought you here, to Buckholme House?"

"That's complicated…"

"No backing out, Six. I told you about my boyfriend's S.T.D, it's only fair."

Six picks up his coffee cup, takes a long drink and then nods his agreement. "Fair comment, Four. I guess it's quite cliché, really. I met a woman and moved to New York to be with her. I had a restaurant that was doing okay, and then my fiancée shagged my headwaiter. We broke up, they got together and let's just say the city lost its charm for me." Six takes another slug of his coffee, his eyes measuring my reaction.

"I guess heartbreak will take the shine off a place…" I glance around my apartment. It could do with a freshen up, but I still love it just as much as the day I got the keys, further evidence that my heart was not broken by Chris.

"My heart wasn't… Four, I'm a successful, self-assured guy. I was annoyed, yes, but heartbroken, no. Gabby wasn't the girl for me. My mum got sick and truth be told, when shit goes down, you sometimes realise home is where the heart is." Six finishes his coffee, deep in thought.

"Is your mum okay?"

"She died of breast cancer. I think you might have seen me the night of the wake; I was a little... out of sorts." I think back to the night of his sexy dance, the night Twenty comforted him, or did she just take advantage of him? I also remember what a cow I've been to him since.

"Six, I'm so sorry. I... I haven't been kind to you had I known I would have..."

"Baked me some cookies?" Six laughs. "It's okay, Four. Frankly, you've been some light relief during a dark time; a pleasant distraction."

"Was Twenty also a pleasant distraction?" I ask and immediately wish I could drag back the words and pop the green-eyed monster back in her cage.

"I guess she was... of a different kind."

I'm trying to work out exactly what that means when the front door slams against the wall and a familiar voice sings, "Hello, hello, Nurse Melinda is here to beat you to death for not answering your phone!"

Melinda walks in loaded with grocery bags and a bunch of yellow tulips. "For the invalid!" she says and dumps the bags on the coffee table. Six is able to rescue his cup just in time. "Right, I've brought you soup, bread, milk, coffee—the good stuff—not that crap you buy, eggs—from the happy hens in my garden, bacon—from the unhappy dead ones at the abattoir—hopefully the pigs won't haunt you, and I picked up some more painkillers. How is the patient?" Melinda checks with Six, not me.

"Impatient and whiny but less so than yesterday," Six says, grinning to Melinda.

"I am not whiny! I have a serious injury and can barely walk. Not that you would know for all the sympathy it's gotten me."

"I did warn you she'd be whiny. When she had her tonsils out, she moved in with me. Joanie has a lower pain threshold than my two-year-old. Thanks for taking care of her. Have you eaten?"

I explain that we have, and Melinda turns into a tornado, dusting and cleaning and making fresh coffee. As she sips her own coffee, she chats and sends texts and emails. Then, she puts my laundry in the machine and appears in the lounge, holding my phone.

"What was this doing in your laundry basket?" she asks.

Six eyes the device carefully and then looks at me with a grin spreading across his face.

"Well, you see, I um..." I try to explain, but my mind is consumed by the knowledge that there is a very naked picture of a very hot Six on that phone. Thank God it wasn't washed clean.

"It was very dirty, wasn't it, Four? Filthy, even. Wouldn't you say?" Six says looking from me to the phone.

I bite my lip and close my eyes. It's as if wherever Six is, my humiliation is not far behind.

"You two are weird," Melinda says, putting my phone on the coffee table.

Six takes the phone, presses a few buttons, handing it to me and quietly, just to me, with a waggle of his eyebrows, says, "In case you miss me or you need something sexy to look at. I've added my phone number." Then he calls out for Melinda's benefit, "I'm going to head into work if you guys are okay?"

"Of course, you should get back to work. Thanks for staying with me." Suddenly I don't want him to go. "Six," I say as he turns his back to leave. He turns to face me as Melinda stocks my fridge. "Do I get to know your name yet?"

"Soon enough, Four. Soon enough."

He gives me a sexy little grin, takes out his phone, and snaps a picture of me.

"Six!" I yell.

Six laughs as he opens the door.

"Fair is fair, Four," Six says as the door slams shut

behind him.

The smile beams from my face, and all I can think about as I light up my phone and scroll to my photos is when I will see him, this naked and in person again.

***

"All sharp items have been removed from the proximity and it is safe to enter. Repeat. Safe to enter," Melinda squawks into her phone.

"What are you up to?" I ask, cringing at the thought of another date.

"Mikey is on his way in. He's ready for you to apologise for eating his cookies, and I think it's time you guys made up."

The door opens and in walks Mikey like he owns the place, wearing jeans so tight and skinny you can see the flex of his thigh, and a coat so light and fluffy, I'm wondering if Big Bird got highlights.

Damn Mikey for making Big Bird look cute!

"I'm not apologising," I tell Melinda.

Mikey drapes his coat over the sofa and sits in Six's chair, folding his arms over his pale blue shirt. "I'm not apologising either. She stole my cookies!" Mikey tells Melinda.

"He cooked drugs in my apartment!" I yell to Melinda.

"She stole from me!"

"He sent me on a date with a police officer, STONED!"

"She almost ruined my date with Chef! I spent the first hour saving her greedy ass!"

I turn to Mikey, incredulous. "I am not greedy! I've lost two pounds this week."

Mikey turns right to me, his features cross. "I didn't say you were fat! I said you were greedy. I cooked you your own batch, which, by the way, I made especially for you."

"I know. I ate the whole container when I came back

from my date with the police officer, stoned!"

"Were they any good? It was a new recipe."

"Delicious, but that is not the point!"

"Both of you—STOP! You are both to blame. Mikey, you do not prepare drugs in someone else's apartment. That is not cool! Joanie, you need to be more careful what you put in your mouth! Got it? Now apologise to each other," Melinda yells.

We both stop and look. Melinda's hands are in the 'T' shape that she uses to timeout the kids. I sigh. Arguing is exhausting and I really want to get both their opinions about my latest encounter with Six.

"I'm only apologising if he makes me cookies, minus the pot."

Mikey grins and cocks his head. "Already have." He reaches down to his bag and pulls out a familiar looking container. "No pot this time, I promise. Moreover, I am sorry. I should have known you'd have stolen them."

I nod. "Then I'm sorry too."

Melinda claps her hands and we tuck into the cookies. "Did you hear back from the police man? I take it he doesn't want a second date with me?" I laugh.

"No, he said you were a little 'eccentric' for his tastes."

"Totally better than being called a 'Plain Jane' though, right?" Mikey chips in.

"Who called me a Plain Jane?" I ask, feeling a little hurt.

"Brett. He said you were probably a bit tame for his wild ways. Wayne thought you were a bit vanilla for his tastes, also."

"What? Are you kidding me? Brett wanted to drunk drive me all the way home!"

"I bet he did, you saucy gal!" Mikey sniggers teasingly and I shake my head.

"Wayne started touching himself on the video call. Seriously, Melinda, where the hell did you find these guys?"

"They were all the available bachelors I could find at short notice. Date eight, nine, and ten are much better, though. I'm giving you until Friday to recuperate and then you are back in the game, my dear Joanie."

"Actually, I wanted to talk to you about that. I..."

"Don't you dare back out now Joanie Fox. I survived cookery one-oh-one!"

"I broke my ass!"

"I met Chef and I really like him."

Melinda and I swing our heads at this revelation.

"He's... well he's a bit Gordon Ramsey on steroids, and... Well it's early days, but I'm seeing him again tonight."

Melinda and I bounce excitedly until I howl in pain.

"Pain in the butt?" Melinda checks.

"Uh-huh."

"Here, take some of these. You need to be at your best for Friday. You have another date!"

"Melinda, no. Really... I... what the hell... I snogged the face off Six. But I'm not sure he's looking for anything serious. He said I was a 'pleasant distraction,' whatever that means." My mouth turns down at the sides and I wonder where I stand. "What if he just sees me as an eccentric, Plain Jane with a cookie habit?"

"He said what? A pleasant distraction? Is he fricking kidding me? I am sick and tired of men who think they own the place, cluttering up the world with their thick-ass comments. Thinking they can come and go as they please, and that you will do the dishes and feed the kids while they go around shagging twenty-two-year-olds. WHO do they think they are? Charlatans, that's what they are! In a few years, they'll be bald and fat and who'll be laughing then? Us. That's who." Melinda's eyes tear up. "And now I've got sodding mascara in my eye. See what total bastards men are. Not you Mikey, you're a doll..."

Mikey hands Melinda a tissue and we both stand there, wide eyed, watching our best friend, stronger than He-

Man, break down.

"Shit. It's true then. Steve cheated?" I ask, willing it all to be a big mistake.

"It's been going on since the spring. While I was teaching Teeg to ride her bike, Jakey was learning to fish, and Ed was still trying to hang off my tit every five-minutes of the day, Steve was boning the barmaid at the Dog and Duck!"

"Oh Melinda, what a bastard!" Mikey calls it as it is.

"I know. What other child friendly pubs are there within walking distance? None, that's how many! And now I have to keep my shit together long enough to see my four babies into adulthood, and I have no idea how I'm going to do it!"

"We'll help you, Melinda. We're a family us three."

Melinda leaves to pick up the kids from school and nursery and Mikey goes for his date with Chef. I stretch my aching muscles and try walking around the house. I even manage to run myself a bath. As I walk to my set of drawers for clean pyjamas, I hear Six's door creak as it closes.

I text him: Fancy some supper?

It's a few minutes before he replies. When he does, it simply reads: Can't, I'm busy. Rain check?

I reply instantly: Sure.

I don't know what this means, but I shave my legs extra closely, just in case.

Chapter 14

I don't see Six at all on Tuesday. He texts on Wednesday to ask if I need anything, but since Mikey and Melinda are popping in every day, my cupboards are the most well stocked that they have ever been. The only thing I do need can't be bought from a convenience store, not lawfully anyway.

Six hadn't taken me up on the offer of supper and I start to wonder if our connection had just been a figment of my imagination.

By Thursday, I am walking in an upright position, and I'm finally able to put on my own socks. I practice some of the badly drawn stretches noted on the leaflet and, out of sheer boredom, practice playing Six's trombone.

Melinda calls just after lunch to let me know that she has arranged for my car to be delivered back to me. She needs to know where it should be parked. I check out the window and notice that my usual space is for once empty and while this should fill me with delight, it just makes me feel empty and a little bit sad inside. Perhaps I pushed too much to find out about Six and now he thinks I'm too nosey or worse, clingy.

I pull out my phone and look at my picture of Six.

My God, those abs really are divine.

I torture myself some more and wonder if I should text him, but since I haven't heard from him I decide to put all thoughts of Six out of my mind. He was obviously just being neighbourly when he helped me to shower and kissed any remaining sanity I had right out of my body. Now all that is left is a horny, slightly neurotic, nearly middle-aged crazy woman.

I have to keep busy. I switch the radio up high and pull out my decorating supplies. I'm going to paint my hallway battleship grey if it kills me, which it could since I still wince when I stretch and bend. It will take my mind off that bastard Six who is clearly not thinking of me, or else he would have called, texted, or visited me. I haven't even heard much noise from the apartment next door. Maybe he's gone back to shagging Twenty and now all thoughts of Four are long behind him.

I angrily pull out the roller and paint can from the cupboard next to the bathroom and pour a liberal amount of paint into the tray. I start at the point nearest the front door and work my way back towards the lounge, stopping to rest and stretch. I try to start slow and careful, but the sombre shade and my pissy mood soon turns my strokes angry as I smear it against the wall. It's a bit like angry sex but messier and lacking the satisfaction or the relief.

Each time I hear a noise in the corridor outside, I stop and check the peephole, but it's not Six. I meet Two's elderly girlfriend though, and she introduces me to her poodle, Bob, who matches Two's poodle, Sue. I find their double dating with their canines cute, and I realise there really is someone for everyone, even poodles.

Except me, it seems.

I continue to paint everything grey and by the time I am finished, my hallway matches the bleakness of my mood. It looks depressive and dull, and my muscles hurt so much that I actually want to cry. So much for keeping busy and cheering myself up. My hallway doesn't look sleek and modern like Six's; it looks like the inside of Parkhurst Prison.

I pour myself a large glass of wine and start to run a bath. My reflection in the mirror mocks my age and single status, as the grey flecks from the paint stains my normally brown hair.

The intercom buzzes to life and makes me jump. I jolt my back as I rush to answer it. "Hello."

"Got your keys," a crackly voice says.

I buzz him in. At least with my car back I can go out for a few hours tomorrow.

After a few minutes of waiting in the doorway the man arrives. However, it's not the courier service I was expecting; no, of course it's not. It's my date from the paintball, what's-his-name.

Shit!

I quickly shake my hair loose, hoping he doesn't want to stop and make small talk with me minus my make-up. Maybe he'll even mistake me for a grey haired elderly person; I toy with whether I could pull off pretending to be my Granny.

"Hi," I say, greeting him with a small smile. The least I can do is to be friendly since he brought my car back, even if he was partly responsible for my predicament.

He looks identical to how he did on our date, like an Action Man. He's wearing camouflage cargo bottoms and a tight fitting T-shirt. I wonder if he just got off work or if he dresses ready for combat every day. His forearm has a tattoo of a dragon attacking a dog, all gnarly teeth, blood and saliva. I don't like it. It's too graphic and violent. It makes me feel sorry for the poor rabid dog about to be devoured.

"Hi Joanie," Action Man growls as he approaches me. I want to grimace, not really in the mood for a chat, but he holds out the keys to my car on one finger. I maintain a neutral face. The last thing I need is to be carless come

Monday.

"One set of keys. I put it in the space out front and I topped up your oil. I hope you don't mind, but it's not good to drive a car around without it." Action Man chuckles and I thank him, hoping he might just say goodbye and leave me to my bath.

No such luck. He holds the keys, just out of reach, and continues his chatter. "So, last Sunday was intense, huh? I would have called you to check on you, perhaps ask you out for a second date, but I don't have your number."

The keys dangle from Action Man's finger as he stares into my eyes. The pause isn't just pregnant; it houses a dormitory of cadets as he waits for me to respond.

"I um… yeah, it sure was intense. Still feeling the intensity of that attack now, laugh out loud." I face palm, I can't actually believe I said 'laugh out loud.' Still, with any luck, he'll think I'm a complete dork and there will be no more mention of second dates.

I reach up to take my keys from Action Man, but I'm distracted as Six rounds the corner and strolls towards us. He's wearing a sharp navy suit and his hair is neatly styled. He has a forceful look in his eyes that demands my attention. They're narrowed black holes as he glances away from me to focus on Action Man.

Six walks the corridor like a raging bull. Suddenly Action Man looks weak and puny. Just when I think Six is going to storm straight past us, Action Man says, "So, how about that second date?"

My mouth falls open.

Six swings around and stops abruptly in between Action Man and me.

I feel like I've just been dropped in a war zone and debris is blasting all around me. I don't know whom to look at or whether to run for cover.

Then, as if the sun, peeking through a stormy cloud Six smiles and says, "Hi, Four. I just thought I… What the fuck is that all over your face?"

I pick a piece of dried grey paint from my shirt and answer, "It's paint! I've been painting the hallway."

"Oh, you look like you've been rolling around in bird shit. Anyway, I thought I'd stop to check how you are, see if you needed any more help with showering?" Six's eyebrows rise and his tongue gives a sexy sweep of his lower lip. Action Man must decide that Six is joking because he gives him a friendly greeting and holds his hand out to shake.

Six blatantly pretends he doesn't see this action, saying, "Oh, hi. Sorry, I didn't see you there, must be the camouflage." Six plasters a friendly smile over the concrete edges of his stony face and turns back to me. "Who's your friend, Four?"

I stand mute, stuck to the spot.

Action Man is still waiting for my answer to his question, and Six just asked me the worst question in the world.

"I um… this is um…" I smile politely, racking my brain even though I know damn well I can't flipping remember his name. I feel perspiration creep down my spine when an epiphany hits me. "This is my date, from Sunday," I say with relief.

That, Joanie Fox, is a perfectly acceptable introduction.

"He just brought my car back. You know, because on Sunday I couldn't walk, let alone drive." I let out a strangled giggle.

Six performs a slow understanding nod. "I see. What did you say his name was?" His voice is innocent enough, but his quizzical eyes and mocking smirk clue me in to his more sinister motive. It's then the penny drops, Six has stopped by to date shame me, and he must know I have no idea what Action Man's name is, not without checking my emails first.

I raise my chin up and stare angrily at Six, ready for battle. Action Man studies us both in turn. He must decide that Six is a friendly if not a nosey neighbour, because undeterred, he interrupts our staring competition to ask me, "So, that second date? I've got a pass for the paragliding club. I can get us both in free." Action Man lowers the arm holding the keys and leans against the door, closer to me, as if he just delivered good news and I might want to thank him.

The horror flooding my mind must be invisible because Six says, "What a fantastic idea. Four was just saying the other day how she'd like to get out more, take even more risks. This is perfect!" He guffaws and slaps his thigh. His eyes crinkle in delight as my fists harden into rocks ready to pound his face.

Now that my keys dangle closer, I'm able to snatch them from Action Man. "Thanks for dropping the keys back. I'm not sure my doctor would agree to any more extreme sports, but thanks all the same. I must go. I think I can hear my bath. It'll be flooding the apartment if I don't get to it."

I leap back and push the door, breathing a sigh of relief as soon as it is closed. I peer through the peephole to see Action Man and Six stare at each other for a moment, before turning and heading off in their separate directions.

My mind wanders into dangerous territory as I question if Six was jealous or just enjoying teasing me. Part of me hopes he was jealous because that might mean he really cares for me.

***

That night, once I'm in my pyjamas and readying for bed, I hear tiptoes in the hall. When I run to the peephole, I see Twenty saunter past in high heels and a short skirt on her way to Six's apartment. She knocks eagerly eight times, the trollop!

Six opens the door and says something. Twenty giggles in response like a hyena that's eaten a machine gun. Then the door lightly clicks as it closes.

Trust Six to make me feel feelings, and then ruin it by
fucking   the   feline.

Chapter 15

On Friday, Melinda and Mikey visit to check if I need anything and I cook us all lunch. Mikey has been swooning about Jamie, his hot new chef boyfriend. He's also complaining about having to return to work on Monday, when he'd rather hang out with Chef; and Melinda has been opening up about Steve and their marital problems. It seems she and Steve have been unhappy for quite some time, and now that they've told the kids about their separation, Melinda's single status has been confirmed. She explains that while Ed and Sunny are too young to understand, Teegan and Jakey were upset, but once she had absolutely promised that this would not mean a reduction in pocket money or having to spend more time with Granny, they apparently seemed okay with the idea if it meant the house was more harmonious and less war zone.

"So, are you sure you're okay? It must be strange without him. Are you going to start dating again? Because I have three dates left and I honestly don't mind you taking them," I tell Melinda, now that her tears have passed.

"No. No dating for me. The only thing that is getting me through this is my sheer disgust at the opposite sex!"

"Hey," Mikey says, offended.

"Present company excluded, obviously. Besides, Joanie, you've got some good dates with decent men coming up."

"I thought you were going to get it on with the hot guy next door. He is fit, Joanie. Thanks to you and your broken ass, I never did get to take him to the mile high club. Seriously though, if I hadn't met Jamie... Hmm, I definitely would." Mikey jokingly performs a dry humping act, making me giggle even though thinking of Six makes me furious.

"Humph, he can go to hell. He came around, all caring and sweet, cooking me food and helping me... around the house and then nothing. Then, last night, last night he has Big-Tits-Twenty over! I'm done," I tell them.

Melinda shakes her head in disgust. "That cheating bastard! We'll show him what he's missing. Tonight you're going out with Adrian Burns. You'll like him, he's loaded and a very eligible bachelor."

"He's the brother of someone I dated years ago; he owns the Country Club up at Fairfield. He's high society, Joanie. You might want to break out the Dior." Mikey winks.

"Shit. I've never been out with anyone rich before. Do you think I'll be okay?" I ask.

"You'll be fine. Just leave your potty mouth at home and wear your best knickers," Melinda tells me.

"It's all about the D.E.M with the high society lot," Mikey advises and I give him a questioning glance. "Decorum, Etiquette, and Manners," Mikey clarifies, picking some breadcrumbs from my shirt.

I nod and brush away his hand. I can totally be D.E.M. I am the height of sophistication, sometimes. Truth be told, he could be the richest, best-looking son of a bitch out there and I still wouldn't feel in the mood.

"Where's he taking her, anyway?" Mikey asks Melinda.

"Some new casino. It's the opening night. You'll want to dress for glamour and put on some heels."

"That's okay for you to say, my ass is purple thanks to the dating schedule you arranged, and I'm still walking with a limp."

"Quit whining. This one will be okay. I'm almost completely sure of it," Melinda says.

***

Melinda told me to expect a limousine to pick me up. No danger of drunk drivers tonight, I hope. I steadied my nerves with a glass of wine and nearly broke my foot when I thought I heard movement in the corridor outside and rushed to the door, only to almost slip and break my ankle on a flyer that had been shoved under the door, probably another take-away menu.

I put on my four-inch-high strappy shoes, even though my right foot looks like it's trying to escape my shoe by means of swelling. Thankfully, my ankle length red dress is just long enough to cover my feet, except for when a whoosh of wind opens the dress at the split that starts at the top of my thigh. I tease my hair into an up-do and put on some bright red lipstick, in an effort to try and fake some enthusiasm.

I wait in the foyer at nine p.m. on the dot, as instructed by Melinda. It's pitch black outside, and the wind rattles the trees causing an eerie scratching sound as if wood is scraping against metal. The light of the foyer blinks, and I'm suddenly aware that whilst anyone outside can see inside perfectly, I can't see anything beyond the double glass doors.

My nerves are on high alert, making me feel like I need to pee, and I'm more than a little anxious that I might see Six, but since he's obviously screwing Twenty I decide I'm over him. At least if I do see him, I look hot tonight, compared to yesterday when I was covered in paint and looking like an elderly lady being propositioned by Action Man.

The limo marks its arrival with an impolite blast of the horn that's so shrill the fright almost causes me to lose control of my bladder. I shake off the urge to stick my middle finger up at the driver and take a deep breath. Three more dates and my life will be my own again. Thankfully then, I can revert to the relative safety of living in my pyjamas, eating delivered food and reading about handsome heroes and beautiful, sophisticated women.

A gust of wind hits me as I walk outside and almost throws me off the pavement. Luckily, I'm able to regain my balance and remain in an upright position. The limo is black, long and sleek, and even though the British weather is its usual damp and blustery crappiness, the driver gets out of the vehicle to open the door for me.

"Ma-am," he says as though an extra from a Thunder Birds movie.

"All right?" I say.

Shit! Must remember Decorum, Etiquette, and Manners.

For the rest of this evening, I'll be an actress. I'll behave like an extra from Downton Abbey. I slide into the limo, crossing my legs at the heels. I smile eloquently as the passenger door slams shut and the central locking clamps down with an electronic grinding sound.

"How do you do?" I say, and turn to face my suitor.

Holy-fucking-moley.

Adrian Burns wears brown leather brogues and a brown tweed suit, which he pairs with green leather gloves and a green satin cravat. However, it's not his heavy British aristocracy get-up that surprises me most. No, what alarms me most is that Adrian Burns looks to be about seventy-four-years-old, maybe older. It's difficult to tell by the meagre light thrown by the passing streetlights. What limited light is shed on his face is quickly swallowed up by the cavernous sinkholes of his wrinkly, leathery skin. His eyes are tiny black beads propped up by a wide sprawling beak like nose. They are predatory in their assessment of me.

Adrian Burns has the look of a serial killer's grandfather.

"Pleasure, my dear." Adrian takes my right hand from the safety of my leg and picks it up to the sliver of his mouth. His thin lips poke out to a hard pout and scrape a dry, cold kiss on my hand.

A nervous smile creeps along my face, and I wonder how I can end this date, now.

I actually want to kill my friends. I keep myself sane by listing in my head all the ways I can dispose of their bodies. Perhaps Mr. Burns here will lend me his gloves and the very large trunk of his limo. Maybe I can even borrow his driver.

"Is that okay, my dear?"

Shit! He's said something, but I wasn't listening. I allow my head to bob a little, to acknowledge he was talking, and I pretend I was paying attention, which I was not. I pray I didn't just agree to go to a fetish club or even worse, to the bingo.

I think quickly. I need to tell him I'm not well. That this was all a big mistake.

"So, um… Adrian," I relinquish all attempts at pretending I am classy, and I put on my least posh voice. "You ain't quite wot I woz expectin'. You bin' single long then?"

Oh, my God, I sound like Eliza Doolittle gone wrong, trying to chat up Mr. Burns.

"My dear girl, I've been a bachelor a long while, doesn't mean I don't enjoy the opposite sex though. I do, very much so. Besides, I feel change is in the air." Mr. Burns winks and his beady eyes trail up the split in my dress. A spoonful of sick catapults up from my stomach, and I swallow back down it's bitter taste.

As the limo pulls to a stop, my heart stops beating and

plummets into the foot well of the car. My mouth is so dry my tongue sticks like Velcro to the roof of my mouth, but still I force out the words. "I thought we were going to the opening of a casino?"

"We are my dear. It's the grand opening tonight."

I look up at the classic, stately building. Never have I been so afraid to enter a building in all my life.

"I... I... thought this was a restaurant..."

Please, let's go somewhere else...

"Oh it is, but it was always intended to have a casino on the first floor. There was a delay in the planning I believe, but that's been resolved and now it's all set up. Shall we?"

The driver opens my door and takes my arm to help me up. I walk on unsteady legs around the car to meet Burns. He holds out his hand but I pretend I can't see it; instead, I rest my hands on my hips.

"Just one minute, my darling." He holds up one hand. "Thank you, Jones."

If I thought my date's attractiveness could not get any worse, I was wrong. Jones hands Burns a walking stick, which he hunches over as he attempts to mobilise across the gravel of the car park of Dizzying Heights.

The limo drives away and I stand there with Burns as he stops on the second step of the entrance to catch his breath.

If I can just make sure Six doesn't see me with Mr. Burns, I mean Adrian, maybe I can survive this.

***

Once Adrian has reached the top of the stairs, puffed on his inhaler and managed to get the strength back in his legs, he asks a staff member to help direct us to the elevator. After all, those stairs might just be the death of him. I agree to meet him upstairs so I can, "Take a slash," I tell him, still utilizing the worst common accent that I can bring myself to use.

I go to the corner of the entrance hall, out of Adrian's view, and call Melinda. Lucky for her, it goes to the answer machine. "Melinda, I just wanted to say thanks for arranging the date with the millionaire." I spit millionaire as if it's a vile and dirty word. "However, you neglected to mention that Adrian Burns the Seventh is actually, seventy years old! Yes, Melinda, I'm on a date with a geriatric person, reliant on mobility aides and inhalers! You are in so much trouble!"

"Oh am I now, I look forward to finding out exactly what that entails," a smooth voice whispers into my neck causing my knees to wobble.

"Six, fancy you being here." I giggle uncontrollably.

Shoot. Me. Now.

My phone pings Melinda's message tone that I never could quite work out how to change.

"Warning, dating emergency; dating emergency. You have two minutes to respond to this message or you will die a lonely spinster," Mikey then calls out, "With one hundred cats!"

I ignore the message. Six gives me a small smile as he nods his head and drinks me in. "I do own this place, where else would I be, Four? I take it you received my invitation, then? You look, breathtaking."

My knees go weak at his description. Six towers above me in a suit so sharp my eyes might actually bleed. His hair looks soft as ever; it's been cut since I saw him last and falls into a neat, dark side parting. I have to remind myself to breathe. He looks so handsome.

"I'm glad you decided to come tonight. It's a big night for me. I've been so busy this week, trying to make everything perfect."

"I… what…" Why would Six be glad I'm here with Mr. Burns for his opening night? "What invitation?"

"The flyer, under your door. I've been trying to catch you, but I've been here early and leaving late. There was some mix up with the roulette table and... well, it's all sorted now. Wait, if you're not here with me, then..."

My face falls. Six invited me tonight. I swallow a lump in my throat. Surely, I can fix this, if I explain.

"I..." The speech I am about to waffle is interrupted by my message tone: "Warning, dating emergency; dating emergency. You have two minutes to respond to this message or you will die a lonely spinster." Mikey then calls out, "With one hundred cats!"

Six's eyes cross to the source of the offensive sound, to my clutch bag, housing my phone. When his eyes return to mine, they house a hard stare.

"Four, are you on a date? At my casino, on opening night?"

"I... I can explain..." I stutter.

Six shakes his head, in anger or disbelief. "Enjoy your evening, Four."

Six turns and takes long strides across the polished floor and walks out through a door marked 'private,' which slams behind him.

"Cooiee... Joanie, I made it up here." Mr. Burns grins in delight, waving his arm in the air from the first floor balcony.

***

When I get to the top of the curved staircase, I'm ready to tell Burns I'm leaving. I don't care if I have to walk, I'm going home.

Burns holds out a glass of champagne and since it would be rude to refuse it, I down it in one. The bubbles hit my stomach, releasing a fizz.

"I took the liberty of purchasing some chips for you," Burns says, taking my hand and depositing five black chips emblazoned with gold lettering reading Dizzying Heights. "Shall we start at the Black Jack table?" he asks.

I'm still enamoured by the weight of the chips in my

hand as Burns leads me through the elegant double doors into the Casino Hall. Every square inch is opulent and classy and matches the restaurant downstairs. A huge chandelier hangs overhead, dimly lighting the vast space. There are green felted tables laid out with cards, chips, and roulette. Hives of people surround the tables and the sound of light cheers and muffled conversations are a mere hum above the singer on the stage crooning a Sinatra song.

Six did good. The casino is busy and the air of excitement is even penetrating my bleak mood.

A uniformed waiter carries a tray of champagne. If I must stay a while, a drink will surely help so I take two from the tray. I guzzle one quickly as Burns hobbles alongside me, and I put the empty glass back on the tray. I then grab another glass for Burns. The waiter is either too polite to say anything or barely registers my lushful behaviour. I then let Burns guide me to the Black Jack table.

Burns tells the croupier to deal me in. I look at Burns and explain I have no idea how to play Black Jack. I've never even been to a casino before, let alone bet. "Just hit twenty-one," he tells me.

The cards are dealt. A six and a four. "Twist." The voice comes from behind me. I don't need to check who it is. The gravelly voice is committed to my memory. The scent of the woody, masculine fragrance is close enough to make my mouth water. I coolly take a sip of the champagne and agree when the croupier checks that I am indeed happy to twist.

The croupier places the eight of hearts in front of me, and the people at the crowded table gasp in delight. The croupier moves on to the next player and turns over a ten of spades. "Bust," says the croupier. When it's my turn again, Six's low voice demands that I twist. Burns suggests that I stick, but I follow Six's advice. A two of clubs is turned over and I bounce and clap in glee. "Yay. I got twenty! I'm winning," I squeal.

It's then that I see Twenty in the distance at the roulette table. She's in a silver dress that makes her look like a malnourished chicken in a roll of tin foil. Even in the dim light and from across the room I can see the outline of her nipples as they point at the ceiling. I turn to view Six, who is looking at me, and then to Burns, doing the math.

"Four, is this senior citizen your date?" Six smirks like a sanctimonious jerk.

The croupier is waiting for my decision to stick or twist. I want to avoid explaining my predicament, which will surely give that bastard a laugh at my expense. Across the room, Twenty is closing the distance between us, looking at Six as though he is the oven in which to roast her meat. I glumly look at my cards as they sneer the total of twenty as if in flashing bulbs and highlighted numbers.

"Twist!" I call out, and there's a sharp intake of breath from the crowd of onlookers.

"Have you lost your mind? That's a one-hundred-pound chip, you already have twenty. Stick." Burns urges from my right and grabs a hold of my hand.

"Gamble," Six says from my left, his finger lightly stroking my arm.

The croupier looks at me to check. Behind him is Twenty, braless breasts are bouncing as she saunters over towards Six.

"Twist," I repeat and take another sip of my champagne. My heart thumps to the beat of the music and the tension is an electrical current on my skin. As if in slow motion, the croupier turns over my card... The Ace Of Hearts. The crowd cheers in delight as I spin and face Six. The smile on my face reaches my ears as I literally leap into him, my arms flinging themselves around him, completely carried away in the excitement.

"I won!" I yell.

Six chuckles. "You did, Four. Beyond all odds, you

did."

"Can I have a word?" Twenty stands to Six's side, a murderous look on her face as she appraises my dopey grin.

Six puts me down and I awkwardly put the material of my dress back into place to cover up my knickers. I bite on my lip nervously, wondering if Twenty is about to punch me for fornicating with her date.

"Excuse me." Six shakes off his smile and returns his facial features to their pissed off, hardened state. "I'll leave you to continue your evening with your Grandfather," he says with a sarcastic smirk.

I don't honour his snarky comment with a reply.

Six follows Twenty across the hall, and I turn to see Burns scooping up the chips and depositing them in his pocket.

Charming.

Chapter 16

I lose three out of the four chips that I have left at the Black Jack table. It seems my luck has run out. Burns winces each time another chip stays with the croupier but pretends that his back is hurting him.

As Burns continues to swig at the free champagne, I start to feel quite sorry for him. He tells me that he doesn't see much of his family. For the most part, he thinks they're only interested in his wealth. I would feel even sorrier for him if he didn't leer down the V-neck of my dress each time I leaned forward or sat beside him.

There's a commotion over by the stage and a crowd gathers as glasses are refilled. Burns and I turn to look as we hear a fork tinkling on an empty champagne flute through the hidden surround sound system.

Twenty is standing on the stage, holding a microphone. She rambles on about her task in public relations. Opening the restaurant downstairs, which has been a complete success and how now that she has launched the opening of the casino, she is looking for further opportunities. She is thrilled with tonight's turn out for the opening and is confident the restaurant and casino will continue to be a triumph. Probably bored of her incessant self-publicising, Six takes over. He makes a brief speech to thank everyone for coming and leaves the stage so that everyone can get on with gambling.

A strange feeling washes over me. My face is grinning of its own accord. I'm truly pleased for Six and can see how proud of himself he is as he wanders through the crowd, paying attention to his customers, cracking jokes, and making everyone feel welcome.

Six appears to enjoy the interactions with the smaller, intimate groups of patrons more than the rapt gaze of the crowd.

Tears prick my eyes. I feel proud of him, even though I have no right. I put my champagne flute down and excuse myself to the bathroom, needing to secure a moment alone.

My face looks pale in the mirror. I adjust my hair, which seems to have tangled its way around my dangling Aurora earring, and take out my pillar-box red, Dior lipstick and reapply it to my lips. Even though I'm on the worst date ever, I'm pleased to have been here to witness the casino's opening night and to see Six thrive. Nevertheless, now I'm ready to go home.

The door to the bathroom swings open and bashes the wall, causing me to jump. My senses are assaulted by the overbearing scent of vaporized marigolds and freesia. Unpleasant memories surface of the faux perfume Chris bought me on our first anniversary.

"Ah, Joanie Fox. Didn't think I'd see you here. Still trying to impress your neighbour?" Twenty purrs from beside me. I don't turn around; I just politely smile at her in the mirror.

"Ah Barb, it's been a while since I saw you too. We must be due for another owners' meeting soon," I say, despising the fact that I'm making small talk with the devil.

"Yes. I'll schedule one, although we'll probably all just veto your plea to renew the doors, again."

My fingers clench around my clutch bag as I put away my lipstick, and she continues her unwelcome speech. Twenty tilts her face to the mirror and admires her fish pout. "I never have any problems with the door. Really Joanie, you could do with working out a bit more, particularly at your age." She tinkles a little laugh. It irritates me more than it should.

I faux giggle back. "Well, perhaps what I lack in youth, I make up for in class." I smile innocently, but my eyes deliberately scan her barely there dress and I turn on my heel to leave.

Twenty smirks and then tells me, "I saw Chris yesterday. He was looking for you. I gave him my phone number. You know, since he's back and he's looking for someone to do the PR for his app. It seems your neighbour and your boyfriend can't get enough of me right now." The smile on Twenty's face is so sickly there should be a trail of ants stalking her.

"Ex-boyfriend," I automatically correct her. I'm about to add that they can have her but my mouth just opens and closes with no words coming out. My mind is blown by too much information.

Chris is back.

"Oh, that's right. He is your ex, isn't he? Back from his travels. When I saw your older boyfriend tonight, I was so relieved for you. I was starting to worry you'd wind up one of those dreadful old lushes, desperate and lonely. I'm pleased you found someone. Even your neighbour was starting to pity you and all your futile attempts at meeting someone." She leans in to whisper as a lavatory flushes from one of the cubicles. "We actually had quite a giggle at the way you throw yourself at the men around you."

My blood boils and steam blasts from my ears. My fists ball and I'm one nanosecond from punching smug Twenty out through the wall when an elderly woman vacates the cubicle behind us.

I start to walk out, but before I do, I lean in and lower

my voice to tell her, "Barbie, such a fitting name for a plastic, brainless bimbo. Perhaps you'd be better off eating all that make-up you plaster all over your face, maybe then you'd be prettier on the inside."

I storm out of the bathroom and make my way straight to Burns. My face feels as though it's on fire and the wetness in my eyes is making it difficult to see straight. When I wipe my eyes, I knock out one of my contact lenses. The right side of my world is now blurred beyond recognition, which is only made worse by tears that just won't quit.

When I reach Burns, I find him seated by the roulette table puffing on his inhaler. He has two glasses of champagne in front of him. I gratefully knock one back.

"Adrian, I really have to go," I tell him.

"You're going so soon, Four? Adrian here was just telling me all about his plans for you this evening; seems he really is hoping to cash in his chips." I'd recognise his sarcastic lilt in a room full of comedians. I squint at Six in order to see his face more clearly. His eyebrows rise up and his face hosts that cocky, know-all expression.

I don't know if it's the alcohol, Twenty's revelations, or that I'm just sick and tired of making a fool out of myself, but I put down my glass next to Burns, who looks like he's about to doze off, and turn to give Six the full pelt of my anger.

"You know what, Six, don't. I'm not in the mood. I've heard all about how you laugh at me and mock me. Well, do you know what? Whoever said you were so great, huh? Running around all abs and cocky grin, shagging Twenty and taking the piss out of me." My tears refill my eyes faster than Burns refills the free champagne. As I turn to walk away, my hand sweeps out, knocking over my champagne flute. It sprays liquid right across Burns, who is still sitting beside us looking quite the worse for wear.

"Shit! Now look what you made me do. That's the trouble with you, Six. You're always getting in the way, poking your nose in, mocking! Move out of the way, I've got this."

I push away Six's hand and lean down as I attempt to wipe Burns' leg dry with some paper napkins from the table. I can see Six, out of my good eye, lean back and hold up his hands in surrender. Burns' too close face catches my attention. It's only inches from mine. His eyes probe mine, then his pupils slither like a snake down my neck, to my collar bones down to my… A smile lights up his crinkled face.

"Adrian! My eyes are up here!" I chastise.

His skin tone deepens to crimson and I wonder if he is embarrassed that I just caught him ogling my breasts. I'm about to get up to leave when I notice that his skin tone is darkening to violet and he's clutching at his chest, trying to loosen the emerald green fabric of his cravat.

Burns starts to choke. His tongue hardens and lurches from his mouth and he struggles to gasp for air. His hands shoot out from his chest to grab me and I instinctively leap back, out of his reach. My head spins from left to right searching for help.

"Burns? I mean, Adrian. Are you okay? Somebody do something."

My eyes shoot to Six's and he leaps into action. He loosens Adrian's collar and pulls his phone from his pocket. Six speaks calmly to Adrian, asking if he has any medications, if he knows what is wrong. Adrian clutches at his chest and spits, in a strangled tone, "My heart!"

Six darts into action, dialling into his phone.

"Ambulance, please... Dizzying Heights… Uh-huh…"

Burns hunches over in his seat and his bony fingers scratch at his inside pocket. Six leans down and pulls out his wallet and inhaler. Burns' eyes move to his wallet and he snatches it back, putting it back in his pocket. Six pulls another device from his jacket pocket. He describes it to the telephone operator and then asks Burns to lift his tongue; he explains what he is going to do and then squirts the medicine into Burns' mouth. Burns coughs a little but then takes deep breaths. His cheeks start to pink up a little more, and I'm relieved when he sits back further in the chair and I hear sirens in the distance.

While the paramedics are with Burns, I phone Mikey. Shocked at the turn of events, Mikey says, "I can't believe that he has had a heart attack. Man, he was so fit the last time I saw him, running marathons and winning the Iron Man. Such a nice man, too," Mikey says.

I look over at Burns, who is having his blood pressure taken by the paramedics. His face is angry and pinched as he glares at me. It must have been a long time since Mikey last saw him. Clearly, life has not been kind to Burns during that time.

I explain that Burns will be taken by ambulance to the hospital and Mikey agrees to notify his family so that they can meet him there. Mikey insists on driving over to the casino. I'm not sure I'll be allowed in the ambulance and, as I do not have my car, I have no idea how to summon the limo. I thank Mikey, hang up the phone, and put it back in my clutch. Then I hover. I'm not very useful in emergency type situations, so I let the paramedics do their job and hover around the peripheral edges while Six commands the space and talks confidently with the paramedics.

"Would you like me to come with you?" I ask Burns as he is transferred and seated in the paramedics carrying chair.

"I think you've done quite enough, young lady." He looks weak as he struggles to lift his walking stick in order to wave me back away from him. "I'll be invoicing you for the losses you've incurred for me tonight. I don't think you are at all who Melinda said you would be. She said you were tasteful," Burns scoffs. "More like trashy. It's plain to see you only came here to make this good Samaritan—and damn fool, I might add—jealous. Take me away." Burns instructs the paramedics as Six, who is standing beside me looks on. My head bows and I turn to leave, deciding I'll hide downstairs until Mikey gets here.

"Wait!" Six calls and speeds up to Burns. "That is not how you talk to a lady. She was clearly beyond your measure and had it not been for the unfortunate and misguided intervention of her friend, she would have never have chosen to spend time in your company. I've seen you leering at her and I'm sure our security tapes have too. You will not be invoicing anyone. You will instead thank your lucky stars that you were able to enjoy some time in the company of this beautiful young woman. Or else, you may find yourself barred from this establishment and shamed in the media for your unacceptable behaviour!" Six folds his arms, as though he is serious. I can't help but smile. A masterful Six is a sight to behold.

"She cost me five-hundred-pounds!" Burns is red in the face again and the paramedics, although amused, begin their descent down the stairs.

Six calls after them, "And worth every penny!"

My face reddens. I'm not sure if Six is aware that he just insinuated that I am a very expensive hooker, for the entire casino to hear.

As the crowd looks our way, I turn to avoid their stares and slink away towards the elevator. Six calls after me, but I don't turn around.

What I've seen and felt for Six versus what Twenty has told me are contradictions that I cannot make sense of in his company.

I can smell Six's scent from behind me as I press the button for the ground floor, giving it my full attention even though I can feel the heat of Six's gaze. The door pings open and I walk inside of the empty elevator and hit the button marked 'G.' I hear Six get in too. With my one clear eye, I see him in the mirrored glass. I stay facing the wall and close my eyes, willing the elevator to take the short distance in the fastest possible time.

The doors ping shut and his scent envelopes me. My

mouth waters as I stand, with my eyes closed.

"Four, you've got to stop going on these stupid dates," Six says, his breath licking my neck.

All I hear is stupid.

My eyes open with a pop, one eye crystal clear, the other fuzzy and I turn to meet his gaze. I try to steel my stare but my eyes are traitorous bastards and start to leak.

"It's funny you say that, Six, because stupid is exactly how I feel. Stupid for going on these stupid dates, stupid for feeling so damn lonely, and stupid for thinking you and I were friends when all you really wanted was to laugh at me with Malibu Bitch Tits!"

Six throws me a puzzled look, but I'm too hurt to hold his gaze. The elevator pings open and I launch myself out of it, away from Six.

As I near the bottom of the sweeping staircase, on my way out of the building, I run into Mikey. The tears fall loose as he catches me by looping an arm around me. He stops me and studies my face.

"You poor thing. How are you? I just saw Adrian getting into the ambulance. Shit Joanie, you were meant to be on a date with Adrian the Eighth, not the seventh! Jesus! He's old enough to be your granddad's mouldy uncle. Melinda must have written the wrong number down from my address book."

I stare, open mouthed for a moment. "Wait, he wasn't supposed to be the date? Melinda wasn't supposed to set me up with the, what? Father? Grandfather?"

"Oh my God, no! Of course not. She went through my phone book. The younger one is fit. That one is not. Crikey, Melinda must be losing the plot to make that kind of mistake. You poor thing. I'll take you home. I've baked you some cookies. They'll help make everything okay."

"Mikey, I don't want to get high. I just want to go home and cry into Chesney."

Mikey uses the cuff of his Ralph Lauren sweater to wipe under my eyes. "No, Joanie. No pot, these ones are strictly dark chocolate and cherry," Mikey promises and chuckles.

Six, having caught up to me, stands to my left and greets Mikey. I turn my face away, looking at him hurts my eyes and my heart.

"Mikey, can you take me home now, please?" I ask.

"Give me two minutes, and I'll come with you, Four. You've had a shock tonight, you shouldn't be alone."

I turn to face Six. He's so tall. All narrow waist and big strong shoulders. He's just what I'd pick if I was choosing my ideal. Nevertheless, he's not my ideal. He's been shagging Twenty and mocking me, and even if Twenty's silicone turned to lava and melted her from the inside out, he'd still be unobtainable. Out of my league.

"Six, thanks for helping out with Burns and all, but you should go back to Twenty. She's much more your style," I tell him.

A confused look clouds Six's face. I see Twenty glaring at me from behind Six. "I don't need you." I say the words lightly, but when they leave my mouth, they sound cold. I bite the corner of my lip and link my arm through Mikey's. "I have to go," I tell Six, and lead Mikey away.

On the journey home, a sad feeling seeps into my bones as I come to realise, I've ended it; all the toying around, banter and flirting, it's over now and we can't go back to that. The revelation by Twenty, and my behaviour tonight, it's the final straw.

I've officially drawn a line under my relationship with Six. I decide that tomorrow, I'm putting my beloved apartment on the market. I need a fresh start.

Chapter 17

As soon as I let myself into my apartment, my eyes fill with tears.

I miss him.

He's been shagging Twenty and they've been mocking me.

My tears turn to angry tears. I phone Melinda and pour out my heart by telling her how much I hate Six, and how much I hate Twenty. After Melinda reassures me, I wrap myself in Chesney and cuddle up on the sofa. I fall into a light, jerky, angry sleep that involves running from G-cupped chickens and smothering people with tin foil.

I'm rudely awoken at three-forty-five a.m. by a ferret being fisted; at least that's what the corridor Karaoke sounds like. I leap off the sofa and run to my peephole. Before me is a vision of naked chest and low-slung fitted trousers as Six sings into his beer bottle microphone.

"Call me, call me by my number… call me by my name…" He rocks his hips with the grace of a drunken porn star as he croons and hums to cover the parts of the song that he doesn't know. "I am the one and only…"

I can't help but giggle as Six gives me his very own

performance of my favourite song. His eyes are on mine, through the peephole, as though I am the only girl in the world. He may be drunk, but once he gets into the chorus he's good, really good, and his body's even better.

My face is a huge grin and I find myself miming to the song from the other side of the door.

His volume increases to cover the sound of Two's poodle yapping and Three's yells to "Shut the hell up." Undeterred he sings, only to me, causing goose bumps to shoot up like volcanoes, "You are the one and only."

I hold my own hands and swing from side to side. He's so sexy, I wonder if I should open the door…

No! I should not open the door. He's a player and a mind fucker!

But, I bet he could fuck me out of my mind. Maybe it would get him out of my system? He's so fricking hot. My tongue slips out to wet my dry lips. God, I want him.

I'm going to do it.

I check my hair in the mirror, and wipe the mascara away from under my eyes before throwing one last glance into the peephole. However, Six isn't there.

I open the door, quietly checking up and down the corridor, just in time to see Six being guided into his apartment by a roll of tin foil.

I walk back into my apartment and slam the door.

Trust Six to break my heart without even knowing it was his to break.

***

After spending the night crying, with my headphones on and my dignity off, I get up early and go for a much-needed run to clear my head.

On the way home, I stop by Melinda's. She makes me a strange green concoction using the new juicer that she impulse bought yesterday, and I tell her my cunning plan. Melinda tries to talk me out of it, but I'm resolute. I'm selling my apartment and going travelling. I'll spend some time with my folks, before jetting off to warmer climates. Maybe I'll get a job on a cruise ship or go on a yoga retreat. Perhaps I'll meet a lion tamer and run away with the circus. I just know that I need to get away.

"I need an adventure. It's been a tough year," I tell her.

Melinda reminds me, "You do know that it's still only January, right?"

"Then my mind is even more firmly made up."

"All this because you're in love with Six?" Melinda has the audacity to say this aloud.

I give her the stink eye to make it clear how unwelcome her blasphemous comments are. "I am not in love with Six. Six is a traitorous bastard, who thinks it's okay to steal parking spaces, and sing my favourite songs while partially naked. Six thinks that it's okay to have sex with Twenty. Twenty-Six! Did you ever hear such a ridiculous number?" I ask her.

Melinda shakes her head and I take a gulp of the green grunge, like it's the right thing to do, even though it's snotty texture would probably be best eaten with a spoon.

"I'm not in love with him, anyway," I tell her.

Melinda leans forward in her seat and her lips turn up at the edges. It's the look of a woman formulating a plan of her own.

"So you're going on date number nine, then?" she asks.

"No, Melinda," I groan. "I did the dates, every awful, traumatic, injurious," I rub my butt in respectful remembrance, "...and harrowing date you put me on. Please let me off. I can't take anymore," I say with a dramatic sigh.

Melinda smiles her knowing, placating smile that she gives the children to let them think that they've won.

"Joanie, honey, let's compromise. Tonight we'll go to Mikey's. He's dying to show us his cooking and he wants us to meet Chef. It'll be low key. After all, if you're selling up and leaving, you really ought to devote some quality time to us now, while you still can," she tells me.

"Oh, well I guess that sounds okay," I agree. "Actually, that sounds just what I need."

"Great. I'll clear it with Mikey and pick you up around seven. I'll have a look through the list and find some nice dinner party company."

I gawk at Melinda.

"That's not what I agreed to," I huff and cross my arms.

"Come on, it's just dinner with friends. Steve has the kids and it'll be good practice for me, you know… to get used to guy company again. You'll be supporting me, really," she says. Her bottom lip pokes out and she looks thoughtful. Put like that, I don't know how to turn her down.

"Well, if it'd help you…" I waiver. "Are you sure you're ready?" I ask.

"Oh yeah, it'll be perfect. There's this guy who has a job opening. Steve's getting all tight in the divorce and I'm probably going to need a job, so it's a two bird, one roasting tin, type of situation." Melinda winks.

"So long as you promise there won't be tin foil I'm in," I reluctantly agree.

***

When I arrive home, sweaty and annoyed for allowing myself to be talked into another date by Melinda, I see a huge bunch of pink and yellow carnations, daisies and freesias haphazardly tied together with a straw binding, leaning against my door. Some of them are already starting to wilt, leaving petals on the carpet.

Curious, I scoop them up in my arms and let myself into my apartment where I search for the gift tag. The small brown, innocuous card reads:

Dearest Joan,

The Big Apple can't hold a candle to the apple of my eye.

I missed you too much to stay. I can't live without you. Marry me?

Chris.

As if on fire, the flowers burn a rash on my hands and I run into the kitchen and fling them into the bin. Petals rain down like confetti and I feel as though I'm about to hyperventilate. I close the door to the kitchen behind me and head to the bathroom to shower off the scent of the flowers. As I remove my sports bra and switch on the shower, I'm awash with could-have-beens and wish-had-beens.

I start to consider if Joanie is better off being, Just Joanie, or if there could be a future with Chris, now that he's back.

***

In mild defiance of my non-date, I don't dress up, even though Melinda suggested I wear my emerald green halter neck dress and strappy heels. Instead, I choose a pair of skinny jeans, my brown flat ankle boots and a checked shirt. I wear my hair in a ponytail, push my geeky black framed specs up the bridge of my nose, and fling on a woolly scarf and my Parker coat for good measure. Whatever Melinda and Mikey have up their sleeves, I'm not playing anymore.

Before I leave my apartment, I check the peephole for Six. The corridor is clear, so I swiftly walk out to the front of the building where Melinda waits in her white and battered old SUV that has the look of an old school mini bus.

As we travel to Mikey's plush apartment overlooking the sea, I don't ask about date number nine. Determined to feign disinterest, I keep the conversation going by asking Melinda about her kids. She fills my nervous silence with talk about Jakey's braces and Ed's success with peeing on a ping-pong ball in the toilet. Apparently, he's yet to 'curl one out in the pan,' but Melinda speaks with hope and excitement about the possibility.

Melinda wears a black shift dress with a cute bohemian fringing that sways as I cautiously follow her up to Mikey's apartment. I peer around corners and squint up the stairway as we go. I don't know why I feel nervous, but something in my gut is warning me that all is not well.

"You guys made it!" Mikey opens the door and greets us with a huge smile. Tonight he's wearing an off-white chino trouser and a satin black shirt. I pass him the bottle of Pinot I brought with me and he introduces me to Chef. Chef is close to my height but much broader. He's older than Mikey, with a well-smiled face evidenced by the deep crinkles lining his eyes and mouth. He has a confident, yet friendly smile as he shakes my hand and pulls me in for a hug.

"So you're the unfortunate girl, poisoned by this one's cookie mishaps, huh?" Chef points a jovial thumb in Mikey's direction and we both laugh. "Just one of the many advisories I teach my students; always label the food!"

We all giggle, including Mikey who's eyes are as big as plates as he drinks Chef in with hungry, heart shaped eyes. I can already feel that he is important to Mikey. It brings me comfort knowing that somewhere on this cold rock of misery, two people are happy and in love.

We're led through Mikey's stylish open plan apartment, with its exposed bricks and stainless steel kitchen that up until recently had never been used. The furniture is a mixture of dark woods and bright red textiles, complemented by trendy abstract paintings and sculptures sourced from far-away places.

We're seated at a huge wooden dining table surrounded by comfortable leather chairs of different shapes and sizes.

Mikey has artfully lit the room with dozens of candles and laid the table with fresh white plates and crisp linens. The overall effect is stunning, and I begin to wish I had a real date with someone special to accompany me, as I enjoy my evening with my best friends.

Chef opens a bottle of red wine and explains about key notes and the nose of the bottle. Melinda and I nod seriously and Mikey takes the piss out of us for our pretences. Chef laughs and swats Mikey. Their relationship seems effortless, as if they've known each other forever.

We're interrupted by a knock at the door. I stare at Melinda, and then to Mikey. They both turn to look at each other as though they are innocent little lambs. My stomach turns over and growls like a wolf, warning them that traitorous bastards will be eaten!

Mikey and Chef welcome their guest. His face is obscured by a huge bouquet of flowers. Melinda rubs her hands together and excitedly gets up to welcome the guest too. I sit back in my chair and swig my wine like a petulant teenager just asked to wash the dishes.

"Joanie, your date's here," Melinda sings and walks over to the table, a dark character looms in her shadow. At first, it's difficult to make him out in the candlelight, but I soon recognise the six-foot two, gentle giant and throw my arms around him.

"Donnie! Oh my God, how are you?" I ask. Donnie hugs me tight and lifts me as I pounce on him. "It must have been… shit how long has it been?"

"Ten years," we both say in unison as Donnie puts me down and holds me out to take a good look at me. "It's so good to see you," I say.

There's a knock at the door and Melinda goes to answer it while Donnie and I stare at each other smiling.

"It's good to see you too. You look so fit now, are you still managing the gym?" I ask. The gym is where we all met. Melinda was the PA to Donnie, the boss of a national chain of gyms and I worked in accounts. Mikey didn't work for Pure Fit, but he came in as regular as the staff to ogle the hot bodies and to work on his six pack. We quickly bonded over our love of Tuesday night Yoga followed by Pinot Noir.

"Yep, still managing the gym. Can't you tell?" Donnie grins and quickly tenses all the muscle groups in his arms and chest, which are covered by a tight, white polo shirt. There is no mistaking that Donnie is one hot piece of ass. Although, I'm confused as to why Melinda has chosen Donnie as my date. He's gay as the day is long, not that you'd know.

I let out a laugh, interrupted by a throat clear. I look to the source of the deep cough and am met with Six's hard stare. I glance from Mikey, who looks on the brink of snorting a laugh, and Melinda who casually winks.

"Joanie, this is my dinner guest…"

"Six." I finish her sentence for her as my brain tries to work out what the hell is going on.

Chapter 18

"Four," Six acknowledges me and then looks from me to Donnie and then back to me again. Donnie wraps one arm around my waist as he holds his other arm out to shake Six's hand.

"Good to meet you, man," Donnie says.

Melinda grins and chews on her lip as Donnie continues to hug me close to him.

"So, how long have you wanted to date Six?" I ask Melinda, wondering what she is playing at.

"Oh, I'm not dating him, silly. I just wanted to invite him, you know, to thank him for looking after my friend when I couldn't be there, and also, what with you leaving soon, I thought it'd be good for me to meet new people."

"Oh. Uh-huh. I see," I say. It's lucky that Donnie has a hold of me or else I might be inclined to throw a wobbly.

"She's leaving?" Six asks, but we both ignore him.

"A word, please, Joanie. Let's leave these boys to talk. I could use some help in the bathroom," Melinda says.

Inside the bathroom, Melinda hisses, "Right. Donnie's going to do his straight routine and make Six jealous. You are going to be your usual charming self and make that nitwit jealous, okay?"

I gawk at Melinda. "That's the most ridiculous plan I've ever heard. He's shagging Twenty for God's sake!"

"No. He's not. I asked him. She's just his hired PR."

"What? Unless PR stands for personal Penis Rubber, then I think you're mistaken. I've seen them. She's always coming over, putting him to bed," I tell her.

"He said they haven't, and I believe him. Now get back out there!"

"It's not like I have a bloody choice now that you've ambushed me!" I whisper-yell at Melinda.

"Get over it and man up!" She deadpans.

Melinda and I sit in the two seats that have been pulled out for us on the same side of the table. I sit beside Donnie but notice too late that Six sits opposite me. Mikey serves the plates of food and chef tops up our wine glasses.

"Tonight we're having Stilton crusted fillet steaks with a port and wine sauce," Mikey announces proudly. Chef rubs his back as if to congratulate Mikey's effort.

The food looks and tastes amazing. Mikey is a perfectionist at all tasks in life and as such, he has excelled in making the plate a sheer work of art. As we all tuck in, Melinda encourages a 'go around' in which we all introduce who we are. It's as if we are all on one of those awful team building exercises, but we're all too scared of the boss to refuse.

When it comes to Six's turn, he explains that he's a casino and restaurant owner, who has recently moved back to the UK from the States. When Melinda asks him out right if he is currently single, he confirms to her, while looking at me, that yes he is in fact a single man. I guffaw at his audacity.

"Is there something you'd like to add, Four?" he says, noticing my cynicism.

"No, nothing. Nothing at all."

Six nods and takes another bite of his steak. The table

goes silent for a moment and then Six pipes up. "So, Four. Tell us about the ten dates. Donnie must be number nine?" Six smiles at Donnie.

"I don't want to bring that up," I say, dismissing him.

"Oh that's a shame, it's such a brilliant dinner party story, wouldn't you agree?" Mikey starts snorting and I kick him under the table. All of a sudden, Chef and Donnie are leaning forward, encouraging me to go on. I push my glasses up my nose and throw an especially harsh four-eyed stink eye in Six's direction.

Under duress, I begin, intending to keep my description brief. "Well, Melinda thought that statistically if I dated ten guys in ten days, one of those wouldn't be awful. However," I smile at Donnie, "present company aside, every single one has really been quite awful." I glare at Melinda.

Mikey fizzles with giggles, spitting out his wine and catching it in a napkin as he hammers the table. "Oh my God, Joanie, tell them about Burns, you have to tell them about the heart attack."

I kick Mikey under the table again, but this time he loudly groans and bends to rub at his shin. Everyone at the table looks at Mikey, whose vision stays fixed on me.

I quickly mouth the word sorry while doing a cutthroat action with my finger to warn him against continuing on this path. Mikey smiles sweetly and continues, "Sorry, sciatic flare up. Where was I, oh of course, Joanie's best placed to tell this story."

I purse my lips, wondering where to start. "Well, it wasn't really a heart attack…"

"Yes, it was a heart attack," Six interrupts.

"No, it wasn't," I repeat, throwing a stern look to Six.

"Well, I have a first aid report at Dizzy's that says otherwise," he adds.

Trust Six to throw first aid reports around like he's suddenly a Cardiologist.

"Well, whatever it was, he obviously wasn't very well,"

I say firmly.

"He was fine until he got a look at your tits; his heart gave out there and then," Six says.

"They are great tits," Melinda adds.

"Here, here," Six agrees.

"Can you both stop discussing my tits as if they're not even in the room," I ask.

"Sorry, Four, you were saying."

"I was saying, before I was rudely interrupted, that he wasn't well, and off he went in an ambulance."

"After you gave him a heart attack by putting your tits in his face," Six says with a teasing grin.

"Six, will you please leave my tits out of this. I think it was more to do with you causing a scene."

"Yes, there was a scene, what was that all about..." Six rubs his chin as he ponders, "Ah, I remember now, you saying something about me shagging Twenty, which I have never done, by the way, and mocking you. Four, I would never mock you. Not without your presence, anyway. Where would be the joy in that?"

"If you say so," I say, narrowing my eyes.

"Joanie, tell them about the paintballing," Mikey says with excitement.

"No, I am not talking about the ten dates anymore; it's rude." I say and look lovingly toward Donnie, for effect, who doesn't notice because he is texting on his phone. When I nudge him, he finally catches me looking and puts down his phone, resting his hand on mine.

Six's eyes demand my attention by burning a hole in my retinas. "Why don't you tell us about the proposal by Interflora," he asks.

My face freezes, expressionless, as if a stunned cow ready for the slaughterhouse. I haven't told anyone yet. I couldn't when I haven't worked out what to do about it.

"How did you... um..." I stutter out a response.

Melinda looks from Six to me, waiting for an explanation.

"Did you read the card?" I direct my anger at Six. "Well aren't you the peeping Tom all of a sudden," I say.

"You were out. I was home and I was asked to sign for the delivery by the courier. They couldn't get through the foyer door. The card practically fell on my lap. How was I to know it would be a marriage proposal?"

Typical, suddenly I'm not the only one who can't open the door.

"Who was the card from, might I ask?" Melinda asks and everyone at the table leans towards me as if pulled by magnets.

I fork a big helping of steak into my mouth and mutter a coughed answer.

"Chris? What, when? You can't!" Melinda yells.

I continue chewing, waiting for Melinda to calm down, before finally swallowing and taking a sip of wine before breaking the news. The rest of the table has also given me their undivided attention.

"So, Chris texted me, he wants to meet up with me, to apologise and explain."

"And propose?" Six asks. He has that funny little tick again in his jaw.

"I'm just going to hear him out. You know how passionate he is about his app. He says he just lost sight of the things that are also important to him."

"You cannot be serious! Passionate about his app, more like desperate to get his doormat back! Besides, I thought you were seeing the estate agent, selling up and leaving your best friend when she needs you most."

Melinda looks angrier than I've ever seen her before, even angrier than when Steve broke the dishwasher. Six's eyes are fixed on mine, everyone else looks around the apartment awkwardly avoiding getting dragged into our spat.

"Melinda, I'm sorry, I didn't think." Melinda has never needed anyone, but she's right, she needs me right now. I can't possibly go travelling. I'm not sure I ever really wanted to. I just couldn't bear the thought of watching Twenty come in and out of Six's apartment a second longer.

"I didn't actually think you'd do it, but you're considering it, aren't you? Forget it, I'm fine."

"I'm not going travelling. I'll stay local, maybe I'll get one of those little houses on that estate up the road. Maybe I'll get a dog, Two's poodle is having puppies," I tell them.

"Who's up for pudding?" Mikey deftly changes the subject.

There's a tense atmosphere for the rest of the evening. Melinda paints on a smile but I can feel her hurt. I just don't get a proper chance to apologise. I feel Six staring at me, but when I turn to look he looks away and Donnie makes his excuses and leaves early. At the end of the evening, Melinda asks Six to drive me home, excusing herself with a headache.

I thank Mikey and Chef for their hospitality and Six and I turn to leave. I wave off Six's offer of assistance to get in the car, and we are quiet the whole way home, even though the air is charged more fiercely than the engine of Six's car.

Six walks with his hands in his pockets and his eyes pointing down towards the carpet as we walk through the foyer and along the corridor to our respective apartments.

"So you're really going to meet with the dickhead that broke your heart?" he asks me, looking dejected. Maybe he's just tired from a long evening.

My eyes moisten as I ask, "What's it to you, Six? I know you seem to enjoy teasing me, but it really hurt to find out that you laugh with Twenty about me. What have I ever done to you to deserve to be the butt of your jokes? She slept with my boyfriend, Six. You couldn't have picked anyone worse to laugh at me with."

There's a lump the size of Two's poodle in my throat as I pull out my key, ready to say goodbye to Six.

"I don't laugh at you, not with her, or with anyone. The only time I laugh lately is when you are right beside me. Joanie, she did the PR for the restaurant and then the casino. She occasionally came to the apartment on business, and yes, she put me to bed when I was too drunk to tell her to go home, but I wouldn't ever laugh at you, and I never slept with her. I wouldn't ever want to hurt you in that way. In case you hadn't realised, even though I've been trying to catch your attention, I think you're pretty amazing."

Six pushes his soft dark hair out of his eyes. His face looks serious as his eyes rise up from the floor to meet my gaze. Our eyes lock and I'm lost in the depth of his sincerity.

Six steps forward and lightly cups my face. He wipes away a stray tear and brings his mouth crashing down on mine. The skin on skin contact sets fire to my inhibitions and I throw gas on the flames. My hands go up into his hair and I grip and pull him down onto me. My body heats and pulsates, and my right leg shamefully wraps around Six's thigh. He is reciprocal to my physical suggestion and hoists me up in his arms. My legs wrap around his waist, delighted to have gotten purchase on their goal, and Six leans me back against my door.

I'm consumed by Six's touch as he supports me by holding my ass. The pressure of his lips on mine sends lightning bolts of pleasure down my whole body. When Six breaks our kiss to nibble and taste the delicate skin of my neck, a throaty groan escapes my mouth.

"Shit, Four, I've had a hard-on for you since the first time I saw you..." he says in a raspy tone.

Knowing I need more, with my key still in my hand, I push it towards the lock. The lock must want this as badly as I do, because the mechanism turns with ease and the door swings right open.

Still hitched on Six's waist we bounce along the hallway and into my bedroom. Six lowers me down onto my bed and his jacket is off and on my floor in seconds. Our hands are everywhere, undressing ourselves, and each other in a tangle of hands and fingers. Six peels my jeans off more slowly, standing back as he tosses them on the floor near my door. He sizes me up, as he stands in just his jeans, with his chest gloriously bare. I lean up on my elbows from the bed in only my black bra and knickers.

"Why don't you come over here, Six," I ask, desperate to feel his delicious weight on me.

Six steps towards me, slowly leaning down to kiss me, and then he breaks our kiss to say, "Call me Ryan."

I'm about to turn that information over in my head but am distracted by the unhooking of my bra and the press of his lips on my breasts. His other hand slides down my stomach and slips my underwear down. I tug at his jeans and he removes them completely until there is only soft cotton boxer briefs between us. His skin feels delicious against mine, and my body rocks against his.

A frenzied need detonates inside of me, but as usual, he is one-step ahead of me, already massaging me, building my pleasure to unbearable heights as my fingers dig into his shoulders and his mouth reclaims mine. My hands wander of their own accord and before long they wrap around their goal. I'm quickly able to confirm that I was right; he is hugely hung. He takes a condom from his silver box at the side of my bed and I watch with a greedy hankering as he removes his underwear and prepares himself. My need is acute, to the point of pain, as he leans over me and kisses me with such abandon my hips instinctively buck to meet his. When he presses inside of me, I'm driven crazy and a feral gasp leaves my lungs as he builds a delicious friction from inside out. My groans echo through the room as his pace quickens, intensifying my need.

Just when I think I can stand no more, I'm rewarded with the most delicious release and as I come, I scream:

"Yes, yes, oh—RYAN!"

Chapter 19

When I wake, the first thing that I notice is a delicious ache in my flesh and a mischievous, knowing grin that just won't quit as my mind wanders back to the four, yes four, incredible episodes of getting to know Ryan and Joanie.

I stretch out my legs and arms, wiggling my toes and my fingers back to life. Everything feels disconnected and spongy, like I'm floating on a cloud, unable to anchor myself back to earth. It's a wonderful feeling.

From beside me, Ryan snuffles quietly in his sleep as he lies on his back with a peaceful smile on his face, and I relax in the crook of his arm.

I don't want this moment to ever end, and I'm afraid of what may happen when he wakes. Will we continue where we left off, or will Ryan go back to spending time with Twenty? I'm not sure, but I know I can't bear to find out if it's the latter.

Too soon, we're interrupted from our bedded bliss when the intercom sounds three swift blasts from the hallway. Ryan, still exhausted, sleeps right through it, so I slip on his shirt and walk to the hallway to answer whomever it is.

I say a quiet hello and sniff Ryan's shirt. It smells like home as I wrap myself tightly inside it.

"Hello," I sing again as I wait for an answer. After a few minutes, I start to get annoyed for being dragged out of bed for nothing. I hear Two's dog barking in the distance but no other noises besides that. I leave the intercom and decide to go make Ryan a coffee, perhaps the caffeine will bolster his strength and we can continue the bedroom gymnastics a little longer.

As I'm pouring the coffee there's a knock at the door, and I skip to answer it before they knock again and wake Ryan. Whoever it is must have been let through the foyer door to get this far.

"Joan, babe. God you look amazing. I've missed you!" Chris, his face partially obscured by another large, cheap looking bunch of flowers, says and walks around me, straight into my apartment. "I'll just put these in some water. Good, you're making coffee…"

I'm still holding the door open, my feet, as if rooted to the ground, don't want to move. I can hear the tinkle of spoons and the sound of the refrigerator door open and close. My feet fly into action and I sprint down the hallway and launch myself into the kitchen. I need to get rid of Chris, before Ryan wakes up.

"Whoa there!" Chris catches me around my waist as I enter the kitchen. "Hey, I've missed you too. There'll be plenty of time for all that later, let's have a coffee first. You can help me move my things back in later, and then tonight we'll celebrate."

Chris lets go of me and moves to the counter. It's like he never even left as he hangs his coat on the cupboard door and sips coffee from Ryan's cup. Chris is wearing the Ralph Lauren shirt I bought him for Christmas and the cheap, imitation sports trainers his dad bought for him. He smells of his favourite aftershave, the one that brings out my hay fever. I can already feel my eyes starting to itch.

"Not sure about this coffee, Joan, think we should

probably go back to buying our usual brand," he says, as he looks through the pile of mail on the counter.

I snatch the mail out of his hand.

"Chris, what are you even doing here? We broke up. You need to go. You can't just turn up here when you feel like it."

Chris looks shocked that I took the mail, and his eyes widen like a hurt puppy. He puts down his coffee and holds out his hands, placing them on my wrists.

"Joan, baby, we're made for each other you and I. New York wasn't interested in the app, damn fools! And, it's like really expensive to stay out there. I was out of money in no time at all. It's then that it hit me. You. I missed you. I packed my things straight up and got on the first flight my dad booked for me. I've been figuring everything out, but Joan, I never stopped loving you, just like you never stopped loving me."

A dark shadow catches my attention from the doorway, and I look up to see Ryan. He's wearing my baby pink, fluffy dressing gown, and throwing me a stare so cold the temperature in the room becomes frosty.

My mouth drops open and my head falls to the side. I try to stutter a response, but I'm in a state of shock. Chris notices Ryan and looks from me to him. He focuses on both of us in turn as if the situation is a complex equation.

"'I'm headed off," Ryan says. "I'll see you around, Four."

The air leaves my lungs in a rush. "What? Ryan, wait…" I call after him, but Ryan has long legs, and his path isn't blocked by Chris, whose eyes and nose now appear to be leaking snot. I skirt around Chris and run after Ryan. He makes it to his door and closes it before I get there.

I hammer on the door yelling, "Ryan, it wasn't what it looked like…"

"Oh honey, when someone screams that it isn't what it looks like, it's usually exactly what it looks like." Big-Tits-

Twenty stands at the end of the hall, dressed in her barely there Lycra workout clothes.

I give Twenty a middle-fingured-salute and walk back into my apartment, slamming the door.

***

Once Chris has left, I shower and dress in leggings and a hoody. I curl up on the sofa and instead of wrapping myself in Chesney, I wrap myself in Ryan's shirt. It's lame, I know, but it just feels like the right thing to do. After a while, I receive a text message from Melinda telling me that date number ten will be picking me up from my apartment at six.

Her message is clipped and to the point.

I call her straight back.

"Melinda, I'm so sorry. I should have been there for you, and instead I was spewing on about leaving. I don't want to leave..." I tell her all about my night with Ryan and what followed. I explain that Chris now knows we are not getting back together but that we did leave things on good terms. He even let me in on a shiny nugget of information that I wasn't expecting. Twenty definitely never slept with Ryan. She told Chris that she had the hots for her neighbour but that he was not interested in the slightest. The news made me hop with excitement to have it confirmed in this way, until I considered that the information came too late, Ryan had already walked out. He probably thinks that I'm back with Chris.

"So you see, no more dates, I can't cope with any more. I'm all dated out."

"Oh, babe. Just be ready at six. I'll pick you up and we'll go to the pub, drink, and dance, and just focus on having fun, okay."

"Okay. If you promise no more dates."

"No more dates, babe. You don't need any more."

***

Shortly after five, the intercom buzzes. I forgot that I had arranged for the estate agent to visit to complete a valuation. I buzz him in and wait in the doorway of my apartment.

As the agent walks down the corridor, I notice that he's about my age with dirty blonde hair and a hint of swagger. He wears typical estate agent attire, too much hair gel and a creased shirt and tie from too many hours in a car. He carries a clipboard and a briefcase. I wave to him from my door, and then walk through to the kitchen to switch on the kettle. As I walk back into the hallway to check if he would like a coffee, I notice Ryan standing firm behind the agent, who is looking around the hallway, tape measure in hand.

"Terrible paint job—it will cost a few bob to get that put right," Ryan says from over the agent's shoulder. I grin and shake my head as I notice Ryan is clutching my fluffy pink dressing gown. Seeing him brings a strange fluttering to my belly and a weakness to my knees. "Might want to write down that the place needs modernising," Ryan says and points to the agent's clipboard. "Joanie," he greets me with a stiff bob of his head.

"Ryan," I return his greeting with an equally stiff bob to my head. "It really doesn't need that much modernising," I tell the agent with a weak smile. "Coffee?" I ask.

"Love one, Joanie, though can you use the filtered water, terrible hard water in this block. Better to let prospective buyers know what they're letting themselves in for," he tells the agent.

I take the dressing gown from Ryan and thank him for returning it.

"The water really isn't that hard," I respond. The agent must think we have both taken leave of our senses. "You should check the bathroom. I had a new suite only last year."

The agent goes as instructed through to the bathroom. Ryan leans his head in and tells him, "Might want to note the leaking shower."

"Ryan, what are you doing?" I give him the stink eye.

"Joanie, honesty is always the best policy."

I look at Ryan's kind face. The anger from earlier now smoothed out and he dons a cute smile. A dirty thought enters my head as I think back to the filthy smile he wore last night, which now feels as though it was too long ago.

"You want a coffee?" I ask.

Ryan looks awkward as he leans against the doorway to the bathroom. "Nah, can't stay. I just wanted to return your stuff. I've got to get ready for a date."

"Oh." I nod. I concentrate on stopping my mouth from glumly pointing down at the edges. "I'll see you around then."

"Sure will, Joanie," Ryan says and walks out through the open door.

I go through to the lounge, sit down on Ryan's chair, and put my bare feet on the coffee table, then sniff my dressing gown.

Trust Ryan to start dating on the day that I finally realise I'm in love with him.

Chapter 20

"Wear the red dress. No, not that one. Ah, here, put this on," Melinda yells. My shoulders sag and I begrudgingly pull the dress over my head.

"Please, can we just stay here, watch bad movies and get wasted on wine?" I beg.

"No, we can't. If Six wants to go out on dates, making you all miserable that is his deal. But you, Joanie Fox, are not staying in and staying miserable. We're going to cheer you up if it's the last thing we do! Right, where is your curling iron? Close your eyes and keep your head still…"

Melinda gets me ready with the speed of a well practiced school run and before long we are packed up in her car on our way to the pub.

"Hey, I thought you weren't driving?" I ask, thinking how even more miserable tonight will be without a drinking partner.

"Oh, yeah, of course, I um… I'm just going to leave the car at the pub. We'll get a taxi home and I'll pick it up tomorrow," Melinda replies.

"Uh-huh," I say, trying to muster some enthusiasm.

Melinda pulls the car up outside the Goose and

Gander, which is a pub not far from my apartment. Never mind a taxi; we can walk from here. At least the night just got cheaper. She opens my door and ushers me along the pavement and into the dimly lit pub that smells of stale beer. There's a fair crowd out tonight, but I decide it lacks atmosphere and ask if we can go somewhere else.

"Joanie, the mood you're in you'll be miserable no matter where you go, now—you get the drinks in and I'll find a table."

I trudge to the bar and order the drink I always have when I'm depressed: two Gin and Tonics, and then I order Melinda's Vodka and Coke.

As I place the drinks down on the table Melinda has claimed for us, right in the middle of the bar, opposite the stage, Melinda says, "Look around, there are some hotties here tonight. Look over there."

I look. "Uh! Too squinty," I say.

"Okay, what about him?" Melinda points to her right.

"Uh, too skinny," I say.

"Uh-huh, yeah he is a bit straw like. Ooh, he's nice…" She points to a very young, cherubic guy smiling at us from the bar. He then looks to his equally young friend, says something and then they both gawk at us.

"You should totally go for him, Melinda. I think once he finally hits puberty, you'll have a real catch on your hands." I let out a little chuckle and Melinda joins in.

"See, that's better. There's my funny Joanie. You'll be okay, honey." Melinda puts her hand on mine and my eyes fill up with tears. "Oh, shit, now stop that, right now. We're going to have fun. Oh goody, look, the Karaoke is starting."

"Yay," I deadpan. "Kara-fucking-oke!"

"I'll be right back." Melinda smiles and nips to the bathroom. I utilize the time by downing my drinks and heading to the bar for more. I have to shout my order to the barman as a drunk, tone deaf giant with a strong German accent destroys Kings of Leon's, Sex On Fire.

When I return from the bar with a tray full of drinks, Melinda has returned from the bathroom. I ask her when she intends to start dating again.

"Uh-uh, no way. I'm done. By the time the kids are in bed, I barely have enough energy to take care of my own hygiene let alone take care of business. I'm off men, completely done."

"Mel, you'll change your mind. Perhaps you could enrol in cookery classes. They seem to be the new speed dating if Mikey's luck is anything to go by. Or maybe Mikey and I could put our heads together, come up with a new dating strategy for you and give us a chance to get our own back, huh?" I laugh but Melinda is too preoccupied checking her phone to respond.

"Hmm… Listen Joanie, I'll just pop to the bathroom. Be back in a sec."

"But Melinda, you just went…" I call after her, but Melinda dashes out of her chair as if her sex really is on fire, and is soon out of my line of sight.

I glance around the bar, which really wouldn't be so bad if they added a few soft furnishings, maybe a rug here or there and some grey paint. Most of the other customers sit on wooden chairs and sing along with their friends. A few brave folks even stand near the edge of the stage and bop to terrible renditions of classic songs.

The German giant's torture of our eardrums is replaced by a loud ear-piercing squeal and the DJ announces that the next singer is ready.

I wonder how awful this one will be.

I take a sip of my drink and look for Melinda, wondering too late if I should plug my ears. The opening bars to John Legend's All of Me starts, and I say a little prayer that the singer doesn't desecrate my favourite love song.

I freeze.

I recognise that voice.

My head spins and my eyes widen in shock.

Ryan is singing on the stage.

My mouth is wide open, as I look around, trying to work out which of the other women, who also sit and stand with their mouths agape, is his date.

I can't tell because he is looking at me as he croons. He smiles as I look behind me. He points his index finger at me, to clarify that he is in fact singing to me.

Ryan starts walking towards me, off the stage and across the small wooden area of flooring until he's right near my table. The other people in the pub are looking from him to me as he sings right at me, his eyes unfaltering and beautiful.

Six takes one of my hands in his and pulls me up. He sings the last few notes and wipes away tears that I didn't realise had fallen.

The crowd whistles, cheers and literally goes nuts for Ryan. But I don't see them. It's like they're a far away distraction because all I see is Ryan with his dark, mesmerising eyes pinning me still, sucking me in.

Ryan looks nervous as he assesses my reaction.

I'm still in an utter state of shock. Then he leans in and whispers, the heat of his breath sending shivers all down my body. "Joanie, I do. I'm in love with you. I don't want to see you with Chris or anyone else for that matter, and I don't want you to move, unless it's in with me. I love you." I stare into his eyes, wondering if this is some kind of dream, almost certain that I have not been drugged because the feeling is a million times better than any drug. "Joanie, no pressure but it'd be really great if you kissed me about now. If you want to that is, or else I might have just made a complete Wally out of my…"

I cut off his words as I literally fling myself at him. He takes two steps back and braces my weight as I part his lips and slide my tongue all the way home.

Ryan takes ownership of the kiss and my hands grip his shoulders, letting out a groan into his mouth. It's then that I hear the wolf whistles in the crowd. Ryan gently puts me back on my feet and grabs hold of my hands. He has a sheepish grin on his face as he asks, "Shall we get out of here?"

"Yes. No, wait. Melinda?" I look around, but she's vanished.

"Yeah, um about that." Ryan's eyes house a mischievous sparkle. He pulls me close. "I asked her to bring you here. I'm date ten, your last blind date, I hope. If you don't mind that is? Six and Four do make ten after all…"

I bite my lip to stop from leaping on him again. "Six and Four do indeed make ten. What are your plans for me, now that you've taken me hostage?" I ask.

"Whatever your heart desires, my beautiful, Joanie."

A devious plan formulates in my mind.

"I still have that crossword at home to finish. Six across and seven down are still waiting for our attention, you know…"

Ryan's lips part to form an 'O.'

"Exactly, let's go." I giggle.

Ryan doesn't need to be told twice. He flings me up onto his shoulder and jogs towards the exit.

Trust Ryan to be excellent at crosswords.

Epilogue

6 Months later

Mikey pulls the roast beef out of the oven and my mouth salivates. Lately it seems to do that often.

"Here babe, let me get that for you." Ryan grabs the tray of glasses out of my hands and places them down on Mikey's dining table. He plants a kiss on my head and pulls out a chair at the table. "Sit and rest."

"So, tell me all about this engagement. Go on, I know you're dying to," Melinda says and pulls out my left hand to admire my ring as I sit beside her.

Chef slices the meat and Mikey puts huge trays of potatoes, broccoli, Yorkshire Puddings, and carrots onto the table.

"Well, we were in London on the London Eye, overlooking the city, and Ryan just asked me. No premeditation. No big fanfare. Just two people in love, making a deal."

Ryan sits the other side of me and smiles a mega-watt grin.

"Joanie said yes!" Mikey claps and does a little dance. "This calls for a celebration! We'll have a party; I'll do the food."

"I'll organise the music and guest list," Melinda chimes in.

"Hang on," Mikey says and my stomach drops, wondering if he's guessed. "What's your new surname going to be?"

"Jones," Ryan says proudly.

"Wait, your new name is going to be—Joanie Jacinda Jones?" Melinda smiles, though I know she's dying to crack up laughing.

"You're J-J-Joking!" Mikey spits with laughter. The whole room can't help themselves but laugh, including Ryan.

"Hey—Joanie Jacinda Fox Jones!" I defend.

"It's a beautiful name, baby," Ryan reassures.

"Besides, we want to do it before the baby arrives…" I casually drop into the conversation.

Mikey drops the plate he is holding onto the table and Melinda jumps up in triumph!

"Oh my God, when, how?" Melinda asks, with beaming smile.

"You of all people should know how," I laugh. "I'm four months pregnant, we just found out it's a boy."

Ryan's arms reach around me from behind. He does that a lot lately. My eyes start to fill up. They also do that a lot lately.

We eat a wonderful lunch and I consider how blessed I am, sitting here with my best friends, the people I'm fortunate to have found.

As Mikey and I do the dishes, we plot a revenge that has been a long time coming.

"She'll never go for it," Mikey says.

"That's why we aren't going to tell her."

"How are we going to set her up on ten dates without her even realising that she's on a date?" Mikey asks.

"With very careful planning." I smile and wink to Mikey who high fives me.

"I think that is a brilliant plan!" His eyes are alight with mischief.

Ryan walks towards me and wraps his arms around my waist, planting a kiss on my neck. Even though I've enjoyed a thousand or more such kisses, they still set off fireworks in my belly.

"What are you guys whispering about," Melinda asks as she brings some dirty plates out into the kitchen.

"Trying to talk Joanie out of calling her son Tennyson," Mikey says with a giggle.

"Hey, I like that name," I say.

"Ryan?" Melinda checks.

"Well, it's basic math. Four and Six do make Ten," he jokes, though his eyes are sincere as they gaze down at me, holding me in a caress.

"I love you," I whisper a breathless reply, enamoured by his intense, kind eyes.

Ryan kisses me and rests his hand on my tummy and whispers, "I love you too and our little Ten, forever."

Trust Ryan to make loving us forever be all I ever wanted.

THE END

Novels by Emily James

10 DATES (Joanie's story - Book 1 in the Power of Ten Series)

10 DARES (Melinda's story – Book 2 in the Power of Ten Series)

10 LIES (Katie's story - Book 3 in the Power of Ten Series)

The Mistakes of My Past – A Romantic Suspense Novel

Acknowledgements

To everyone who reads my books, a heartfelt thank you.

To Randie my editor—editorrjc@gmail.com--who took a punt on the underdog and worked her socks off to make this novel better. You are an absolute professional and a total babe. I salute you (and probably owe you some wine and Sangria)!

To Gayle Williams, you championed me from the start, even when I lost belief in myself. You have become a true friend.

To Gina Putvain, who can spot a typo or misplace word from ten paces. More than that, you are beautiful inside and out. Can't wait for the premiere with Channing ;0)

To Saleena Chamberlain, oh my God, I adore you. You were my baptism of fire into the book world and welcomed me with open arms. I always get excited when I see I have mail from you.

To Lucy, you are always my bestie.

To Christina Gamboa who worked tirelessly to support me and thankfully found more right than wrong with this novel. Thank you for your encouragement.

To Jodie Cook, who reads as fast as lightening and always has something important to say, thank you. Check out her blog: https://forthenovellovers.wordpress.com). To Jennifer Bradley, you make awesome effortless and I'm so thankful to have met you—I bloody adore you.

To Felicity Thornwall, who's comments always made me laugh and were right on point (even if I do say so myself ;) you seriously ROCK as a beta and as a person! To Niki Roge @ Romance Filia (check out her blog too!).

I love our time zone and pop culture chats. You just 'get' reading and writing. Never stop!

To Jackie Pinhorn, who just loves romance and spurred me on to get to the good bits already ;0)

To Ellen Montoya, I am so grateful you took the time to help me improve, thank you.

To Andree Schuler, who despite being the busiest lady I know, still found time to help a struggling author—you are a classy and yummy mummy :0)

To Julie Saunders, Nidhi Upadhyaya, Karen O'hara and Sasha Elle.

The kindness you have all shown in supporting and cheering on a new, Indie author like me blows my mind. I thank you for your time and grace, and I promise to always pay it forward. I truly hope that I haven't forgotten anyone. I tend to go a little bonkers after I finish a new book and type those closing words, but please know—I send my absolute love and adoration.

About the Author

Emily James is a British author who lives on the south coast of England. She loves to travel and enjoys nothing more than a great romance story. On the rare occasions that she hasn't got her nose in a book, Emily likes to spend time with her beautiful family and friends.
You can be notified of Emily's future projects via her mailing list:
http://eepurl.com/cpN4t1
Please hit her up on Facebook:
https://www.facebook.com/emily.james.author
Or email her at: emilyjames.author@gmail.com

Made in the USA
Middletown, DE
16 September 2020